TED TAYLER

SILENT TERROR

BOOKS

TED TAYLER

SILENT
TERROR

vinci
BOOKS

By Ted Tayler

The Freeman Files

Fatal Decision

Last Orders

Pressure Point

Deadly Formula

Final Deal

Barking Mad

Creature Discomforts

Silent Terror

Night Train

All Things Bright

Buried Secrets

A Genuine Mistake

Strange Beginnings

Dead Reckoning

A Normal November

Into the Sunlight

Tame the Storm

One True Friend

Whispered Truths

A Morning Murder

Quick to Anger

Red Herring Season
Gathering Clouds
Still Standing

Vinci Books

vinci-books.com

Published by Vinci Books Ltd in 2025

1

A CIP catalogue record for this book is available from the British Library.
Paperback ISBN: 9781036704940

Prologue

Wednesday, 27 June 2018

GROWING UP IN DUNDEE, Lydia Logan's childhood was a happy one. She always knew she was adopted but didn't give it much thought. Her mother, Eleanor Scott, was eighteen when she gave birth to a seven pounds eleven-ounce daughter. The record for her father showed him merely as a Nigerian sailor from Lagos.

Lydia's parents agreed to a closed adoption, which meant few details were made available. Her parents hadn't even known her birth mother's name. When Lydia left school at eighteen, she wanted to be an actress and worked several jobs to fund her classes at Drama school in Glasgow.

Lydia spent years badgering the adoption agency and adoption support groups. While she studied, she spent countless hours in libraries searching the internet. Alex Hardy knew it must have been a tough time for both Lydia and her parents. Despite the loving childhood the Logan's provided, he appreciated Lydia's desire to meet the man and woman who brought her into the world.

Lydia had stayed in digs in term time in Glasgow while she studied, returning home during the holidays. When she reached twenty-one, she moved out for good. The only way Lydia could continue to finance her studies was to work year-round, even if it was part-time. There was no animosity with her parents. Lydia knew she could give them a ring, and her bed would be ready before she'd made the ninety-minute trip back to Dundee.

While she sat in the Mitchell Library searching for a way to find her father, she wondered which occupation might offer the most access to information impossible to unlock online. Lydia hunted for books on forensic psychology and read them to fill in time between internet searches for her father without raising red flags.

Lydia switched her focus to an MSc in Forensic Psychology at Glasgow Caledonian University once she decided this leg of the hunt for her father required a more structured approach.

There were bound to have been pressures on both sides. At the outset, Lydia did not understand why the young Eleanor Scott gave her daughter up for adoption. Was it just the economic impact of caring for a baby alone? The father had disappeared within days of that first meeting, and she'd never heard from again. Inevitably, he never learned he'd fathered a child. Would Eleanor welcome her daughter getting in touch? How would that impact the Logan family if the pair formed a relationship?

Lydia's persistence got its reward in time. The adoption agency wrote to tell her she was now entitled to learn her birth name. Eleanor Scott had named her Lisa Marie.

Armed with this extra knowledge, Lydia then questioned her motives for wanting to continue the hunt.

What if she contacted Eleanor and her mother didn't want to meet her? When Lydia finally plucked up the courage to make that call to Eleanor, it was through a mediator. Lydia stressed that she wasn't asking for anything from Eleanor but was curious to learn more about her. They talked from time to time on the phone for several months before either was ready to meet in person. When they did meet face-to-face, they found it easier to behave as friends rather than attempt to force an instant bond.

When Alex and Lydia got together, she told him what had happened at that first meeting and the information she had gained.

The eighteen-year-old Eleanor Scott worked in a gift shop on George Street, Edinburgh. She started there straight from school. Lydia learned that her father was Chidozie Barre, aged twenty-one, from Yaba, near Lagos.

Chidozie had arrived in the port of Leith two days before he met Eleanor. He was on shore leave for five days and entered the gift shop searching for a memory of Scotland to take home to his mother. The young sailor asked Eleanor to meet him later that evening.

"Chi-Chi, his friends called him," Eleanor had told Lydia. "He was tall and handsome. His smile lit up the shop. I wasn't seeing anyone else, so I thought, why not? When I left work, he waited for me outside. His friends had returned to the ship. We walked to the George IV pub, Chi-Chi bought us a drink, and then we went to the cinema. Please don't ask me what was showing. I can't remember. I told him I needed to get home because my parents didn't know I was staying in the city after work. He was a gentleman. Chi-Chi walked me to the bus stop, and we met the next evening. At half-past five, I came outside the shop, and there he was with a single red rose. We revisited the pub and stayed longer this time. I wasn't a big drinker, so my head was spinning when we came outside. We went to Princes Street Gardens. That was when it happened. I knew he was leaving the next day, and we wouldn't have another night together. It was the first time for both of us. I caught the last bus home and cried myself to sleep. Not because of what we did or because we didn't use protection. It was because I realised that I'd never see him again. My heart sank when I missed that first period. What could I do? I knew his name, but where did he go after he left Leith? What was the name of the ship? It never seemed important to ask. My family didn't want to know. It would have been bad enough if it had been Geordie McEwan from next door. He'd always kept asking for a date, but I was not too fond of the sight of him. But when my Dad heard it was a black man, that was it. I was out the door with my belongings and looking for digs."

Lydia had asked her mother how she'd coped and why she chose the name Lisa Marie.

"The gift shop manager was smashing. She had a cousin with a room for rent, and I worked behind the counter until I grew too big and had to stop. Giving you a name was the only thing I could do before you got taken away from me. Elvis's daughter was pregnant then, and I saw her name in the newspaper that day. I didn't think I would ever see you again, but how hard could it be if I looked for a Lisa Marie?"

Lydia explained to Eleanor how her adoptive parents came to name her Lydia. Not that they didn't approve of her given name of Lisa Marie, or they wanted to prevent

Eleanor from finding her if she came looking. Lydia was her adoptive father's mother's name. It was as simple as that.

So, Eleanor and Lydia kept in touch, primarily by phone. After she completed her MSc, Lydia travelled south for an interview at London Road. Then, she returned to Dundee to visit her parents while she awaited the verdict. They were over the moon when the ACC rang with the news that Wiltshire Police wanted Lydia to start work on April the ninth. Her parents stood on the doorstep with tears in their eyes when Lydia drove away in her red Mini. Lydia was tearful, too, because all three of them accepted that things would never be the same.

When she stepped from her Dundee home on Thursday, the fifth of April, Lydia had just informed her parents she was now Lydia Logan Barre. She drove south to collect the keys to her newly rented accommodation near Chippen-ham, eager to join the newly formed Crime Review Team on Monday. Little did she know that one of her teammates would become so important to her within a few weeks.

Lydia took the train to Edinburgh on Thursday, the tenth of May, and spent the weekend with Eleanor in Craig-millar. Eleanor had lived in that vibrant part of the city for ten years. They spent the time sightseeing and shopping and got on fine.

Lydia didn't want to spoil the mood. She told Eleanor of her new love, Alex, and how much she enjoyed working with Gus Freeman, even if he occasionally criticised her choice of clothing. As she travelled south on a gruelling train journey on Sunday, she thought about what she hadn't shared with her mother.

She didn't tell Eleanor of her attempts to trace her father. Eleanor hadn't forgotten her first love, but she'd moved on. Lydia planned to continue the search for

Chidozie Barre with Alex's help. Her father might not want to see her. But, if he did and asked after Eleanor, that was the right time to ask Eleanor if she wished Chidozie to get in touch. She would leave it to Eleanor to decide.

Lydia and Alex had discussed the next steps they needed to take. First, they had to find the ship he arrived on and where it went when it left the Port of Leith. It was something Lydia said she had to do. She couldn't rest until she found him. It was essential for Lydia to know the man who made her the person she was today.

Alex warned her she wouldn't find it easy to trace Chidozie through Police records unless he now lived in the UK and had committed an offence. Without a valid reason, Lydia couldn't just log on and start searching. Someone would notice.

Lydia knew Alex would do everything he could to help her in her quest. She was glad he was with her today to encourage her to keep going and make sure she did nothing illegal in her haste to find answers.

They had driven to London last night and stayed in a hotel near Greenwich. The Tube journey on the Jubilee Line to the National Maritime Museum took twenty minutes. The person she talked to was knowledgeable, but Lydia realised how challenging this task might be the more she listened.

"How do I trace a ship?" Lydia had asked the Maritime Museum assistant.

"Sometimes, the only way to trace a seaman's record is to trace the records of the ships on which he sailed. You can use the Crew List Index Project website to trace a ship by its name and port of registration. That can help locate merchant seamen in service up to the last decades of the twentieth century."

"Do the seamen have to be British to appear?" asked Lydia.

"Not necessarily, they recorded seamen serving on British registered vessels, but the men themselves need not have been British to appear in the records. Your father visited Leith in the early Nineties, you say?"

"In late ninety-two, that's right."

"It might be better to check the Maritime and Coastguard Agency. That records seamen after 1972. If he was only employed temporarily or was an apprentice, he may not have had a British Seaman's Identity Card, in which case he's unlikely to appear in either register."

"I can still look, though. I want to find my Dad."

"Access to full details of seamen born less than one hundred years ago may be restricted."

"The CLIP catalogues are arranged alphabetically in ranges of surnames. The registers are in eight parts according to the nationality or origin of the seamen and other criteria. It allows for more targeted browsing. You can drill down to what's often referred to as the seaman's docket book. The docket book will show their date and place of birth, rank, or rating. A list of ships and their official numbers with date and place of engagement. It should highlight whether the engagement was for a Foreign or Home trade voyage. Finally, it will include the date and place of discharge from the ship."

Lydia left the Help desk and returned to find Alex.

"Any luck?" he asked.

"It's a shame Gus wants us back at work on Monday," she sighed. "It's a far bigger job than I hoped."

"I'm here to help," said Alex. "We can make a start between now and Friday. If we have to spend our weekends hunting your Dad, that's what we'll do. I know it's important to you."

"You're right," said Lydia, "I've waited twenty-five years to speak to him. Another few weeks won't make that much difference."

Armed with the information Lydia gleaned, the pair set to work on the National Archives. Hours passed, and when the Museum was closing, they realised they needed to return in the morning.

Despite too many drinks in the West End the previous night, Alex and Lydia returned to resume their search by ten the following day.

"It's like peeling away the layers of an onion one at a time, isn't it?" said Lydia.

"You're not kidding," said Alex. "What does your Dad's name mean, anyway? Do you know?"

"I looked it up like an obedient daughter," said Lydia. "May God fix it and make it good for you."

"Right," said Alex, "I might have found something. Perhaps he's fixed it for us. Did you know that refrigerated cargo made up twelve per cent of the goods carried on the seas back in 1992?"

"Before my time," said Lydia.

"Harsh," said Alex, "I was at school, but I wasn't studying economics. Seaborne trade continued to expand despite the downward path of the world economy at the start of the Nineties. One of the major shipping nations back then was Greece, and they remain in the Top Five today. I've found a ship they term a Reefer which transports perishable commodities which require temperature-controlled transportation, such as fruit, meat, fish, vegetables, and dairy products."

"Let me see," said Lydia.

"Don't get too excited," said Alex, "this only gets us part of the way to your father. A Greek ship, sailing under a foreign flag, docked in the Port of Leith between the days your mother mentioned. That reefer was six years old."

"What does sailing under a foreign flag mean?" asked Lydia.

"It's complicated, and it doesn't affect the aim of your search. In simple terms, most merchant ships flying a foreign flag belong to foreign owners who wish to avoid the stricter marine regulations imposed by their own countries. A foreign flag can offer easier registration and the ability to use cheaper foreign labour. Furthermore, foreign owners pay no income taxes."

"What was this ship called?" asked Lydia.

"It carried an Automatic Identification System named CB3 Reefer for location and identification. They built it in 1986, one hundred and thirty-four metres in length and twenty metres wide. Its call sign was 4FKS8."

"Oh, I hoped it had a romantic name such as Ocean Warrior."

"I think the day they started making ships that were longer than a football pitch, the romance went out of sailing," said Alex.

"How many crew members did it have?"

"It depended on the cargo," said Alex, "but my guess is twenty-five to thirty."

"So, we're certain that Chidozie Barre was in the Port of Leith in October 1992 and was working on this CB3 Reefer?"

"It's the only ship listed as being there on those specific dates," said Alex, "So, if the story he gave your mother was correct, then the seamen who visited that gift shop came from that ship."

"Eleanor said he was a gentleman," said Lydia. "He wouldn't have lied to her."

Alex hoped Lydia was right.

"Does that mean their next port of call was Rotterdam?" asked Lydia, pointing at the record on-screen.

"Edinburgh to Rotterdam represents at least eighteen hours of sailing time," said Alex, "if my maths is correct."

"Where did it go next?" asked Lydia.

"That will be another search, I'm afraid. There's no guarantee that your Dad stayed with the ship after Rotterdam. He might have switched to another vessel owned by the same company. I vote we contact the company he worked for on that trip and see if he's still registered with them. He's only ten years older than me, at forty-seven. Chidozie should still be in employment somewhere."

"I looked him up on Facebook," said Lydia, "as soon as I discovered his name. Nobody with that name fits the age, place of birth, and description that Eleanor gave."

"Not everyone is glued to their phones on social media, Lydia. Take Gus, for example. His phone is for making calls and sending messages. Your Dad could be another throwback to a bygone age when people talked to one another."

"Perhaps he doesn't want to be found," said Lydia.

"Come on," said Alex, "we knew it would not be easy. We've made progress this morning. Let's take a break, get a bite to eat, and then ask your friend at the Help desk where to find the number for this Greek shipping company."

An hour later, they returned to the Museum to continue the search.

"Does Gus know what we're doing with our brief break?" asked Lydia.

"I didn't tell him our plans," said Alex. "I remember

biting my tongue one day when we were in his car together. I mentioned you were in touch with your birth mother."

"I bet he was complaining about my dress sense again," said Lydia.

"Not that day, if I remember right. He was commending your innate spirit and the fierce way you present yourself to the world. You always give the impression that you're not taking a backward step no matter what."

"That came from my adoptive father," said Lydia. "As soon as I started school in Dundee, the bullies picked on the ginger-haired black girl. He taught me to stand my ground, stare them down, and get my retaliation in first if they looked like they would hit me. I suffered a few detentions for fighting, but the bullying got less. The racist comments never stopped, though, even when I was studying in Glasgow. The streets can be tough up there, unlike the relative peace in the countryside where we work."

Alex thought, not for the first time, that he was a lucky guy. He couldn't imagine getting through the trauma of the last three months without Lydia in his corner. She'd kept him going when he was ready to quit. Now, although he wasn't free of pain in his body, he had the tools to fight that pain without resorting to pills.

This London trip proved he was on the road to recovery. He had left his stick at home, even if the long lunchtime walk they enjoyed was now causing him discomfort.

"Take the weight off that leg," said Lydia. "Sit yourself down while I find that number."

"If you can read my mind, I must watch what I'm thinking," said Alex.

Two minutes later, Lydia returned with a big smile and a slip of paper.

"Got it," she said. "Will you call them, please? I'm scared of what I might find out."

As Alex made the call, Lydia kissed his cheek and headed for the restrooms.

When she returned, Alex sat holding the phone.

"Sit down," he whispered.

"What's up?" asked Lydia.

"Your father continued to work for this Greek shipping company until 2007. He was no ordinary seaman by that time. He had risen to the rank of Chief Mate for the Deck Department."

"Is that an officer?" asked Lydia.

"Yes, I reckon he would be second in command after the Captain. Chidozie was Chief Mate and prioritised the security and safe functioning of the vessel and was responsible for the crew's welfare on board. His responsibilities included the security appliances and the fire prevention equipment. His most important duty was the safe navigation of the ship. Chidozie was an Officer On Watch for the navigational watches between 0400-0800 hrs and 1600-2000 hrs. The Chief Mate constantly oversees the cargo work in the port. It was a responsible position."

"Why did he leave?" asked Lydia.

Alex took Lydia's hands in his.

"He didn't leave. The Greek-owned vessel carried thirty-seven crew and a cargo of fruit and vegetables when it got into trouble in a storm. The vessel had left Darwin on the seventh of May and was sailing out of Manila en route to China. As CB3 Reefer headed across the South China Sea, it floundered, and the crew battled to keep it afloat in terrible storms. Flooding water made conditions slippery underfoot as the crew fought in vain to save the doomed ship. Typhoon Yutu Amang was blowing when the ship sank. The ship's instruments showed it was sailing into high winds of seventy-two knots or eighty-five miles an hour. The Captain sent a distress call to the Philippine Coast Guard and a general mayday for any nearby vessels to come to their aid. Rescuers in an aircraft and four boats and divers searched for survivors. They found a bundle of orange rope and a life jacket. There was no sign of the cargo ship. When they returned to Manila, they received news that a passing freighter had battled violent, rolling waves to reach the spot where the distress signal originated. They found twelve survivors wearing life jackets and floating in rafts."

"Was my father among the survivors?" asked Lydia.

"He was," said Alex, "but the company spokesman told me that after that experience, Chidozie never went to sea again. At least not with their company. The freighter ferried the survivors to Da Nang, Vietnam, where eight spent the night in the hospital. The walking wounded, such as your father, could travel wherever they wished. After the twenty-third of May 2007, the Greek owners don't know where your father went."

"What do we do now?" asked Lydia.

"Let's get back to the hotel, have a night out in London tonight, and then drive home. We confirmed your father was still alive after that tragedy. Twenty-five crew members lost their lives that day."

"I agree; we need a fresh approach. Did Chidozie leave Da Nang right away? Perhaps he returned to Yaba, in Nigeria, to his family home. Hark at me. I'm assuming he had a family home. What made him go to sea in the first place? Where has he been between 2007 and today? Where do you want to go for your holidays this year?"

"If I could get back on a motorcycle, I'd choose Route 66. I've ticked off most of the European trips I wanted to make. But, given that I would have to travel by car once we got to Lagos, I'd be driving if we did go. You're a nightmare on English roads. Heaven knows what they would make of you over there."

Alex and Lydia returned to Chippenham late on Friday morning. Lydia felt it had been a case of two steps forward and three steps back. Alex convinced her that the opposite applied. They had made progress.

Alex drove to his place on Sunday afternoon. He needed to get things together, ready for his return to work. The CRT night out at the Waggon & Horses had reassured him that Gus and the others would be happy to see him. Any awkwardness would go quickly, probably with a quip from Neil Davis.

As he punished himself with an extra dose of physio to make up for the time off in the capital, Alex thought of what lay ahead for Lydia. There were so many possibilities for what happened next to Chidozie Barre. For a man who had been at sea for eighteen years, what career on land would attract him?

Lydia was downhearted when he left her today. Alex thought she should realise they had learned one more important thing over the past two days. Chi-Chi Barre, the junior rating who stole Eleanor's heart, had battled his way to the senior Merchant Navy position of Chief Mate. She needn't look further to explain why she was such a tough cookie. In the toughest of environments, her father had climbed almost to the top of the pole.

Chapter One

The life and times of Ursula Wakeley 1935-2013

PEOPLE INSTINCTIVELY RECOILED when she called herself a spinster.

But she used the word intentionally and happily because Ursula Wakeley believed such people defined spinsters as often weird, complex, strange beings. She had spent many idle hours in the library in her home town of Mere, defining her version of the modern spinster. One Urban Dictionary entry on *spinster* redefined the term as a woman who can stand independently and doesn't need a man for her life.

"We are living in the age of the single woman," Ursula told a younger colleague.

The shallow smile Ursula received was a typical response from the unenlightened.

Ursula believed she shouldn't get defined by the lack of a husband or children. Those who sneered when she celebrated that she was unmarried and childless either considered her invisible or despised her.

Ursula was born in 1935, the second child of Gideon and Elspeth Wakeley. Gideon was a God-fearing man who toiled as an agricultural labourer until the day he died. Her father never saw the Harvest Festival at the Methodist Church in late September 1966. He dropped dead in the fields a mile from his home on the first day of the month. He was fifty-six. His widow, Elspeth, was two years his junior and needed Ursula at home.

Arthur Wakeley, Assistant Manager at Lloyd's Bank in the town, told Ursula there was nothing to discuss. However, she must give up her job as a librarian and stay home to care for their mother. Arthur was two years older than Ursula and married to Glenda, a former bank cashier. They lived in the town with their two children.

Ursula protested. Why did it fall on her shoulders? She, too, had attended the small school in the town, just like her brother. From the age of eleven, they had made the daily bus trip from Mere, a tiny town on the edge of Salisbury Plain in Wiltshire, to the Gillingham School, across the county border in Dorset. Arthur and Ursula left on the same day in July 1952. Her exam results in the newly intro-duced O-Levels were two grades higher than anything Arthur had achieved at sixteen. Her brother studied three subjects at A-Level and scraped a bare pass in Maths, History, and Geography.

Ursula would have loved to stay on for two further years like her brother. She even dreamed of going to University, but Gideon and Elspeth were adamant. They needed their youngest daughter to bring in a weekly wage to boost the family budget.

"Arthur will marry, and his banking career will take him away from the town," said Gideon. "Your place is here with your mother and me until you marry."

Ursula had started at the library on Barton Lane in September 1952. The fourteen years she spent surrounded by books was the happiest period of her life. She reluctantly handed in her notice within a week of her father's funeral.

Arthur had indeed married and moved to different towns with the bank. Ursula found it ironic that Glenda Simpkins, her best friend at Gillingham school, was the girl Arthur married. When they walked through the school gates together for the final time, Glenda raved about the letter she had received that morning. She had a job offer at the bank as a junior clerk.

"I'll be working with that brother of yours," she grinned. "He's going places, and if I can turn his head, I'll see the country with him. I don't want to stay in this back-water of a place forever."

Glenda never travelled far. She had two children in the first four years of marriage and never returned to work after leaving to await the arrival of Matthew. By the time Samantha arrived, Arthur's career had stalled. He would climb no higher than an Assistant Manager. Rather than move to a manager's position in Salisbury, Dorchester, or further afield, Glenda discovered they were returning to Mere for Arthur to while away the days until he could retire.

No wonder he insisted that I quit my job to look after our mother, thought Ursula. He was bitter. Arthur resented the pleasure I got from my job at the library. And he still hadn't forgiven her for outshining him at school.

Elspeth Wakeley was not the easiest person to live with, but Ursula knuckled down to the task. The years passed, and although she still harboured hopes of a man showing an interest in her at thirty-one, it became apparent that nobody wanted to take on two women.

Caring for an elderly relative can be arduous, and Elspeth made things as difficult as possible. Ursula had never noticed how much of a hypochondriac her mother was until after her father's death. There was always something. It was a release when Elspeth succumbed to a particularly virulent bout of influenza that gripped the country between October and Christmas 1996. Ursula's prison sentence was complete.

"Thirty years," she said to Arthur and Glenda on Boxing Day. "Even the Great Train Robbers never served that long a sentence."

To Arthur's great surprise, the sixty-one-year-old Ursula approached the library to explore the possibility of taking up her old position. They were happy to have her back. After all, she was a familiar face and had visited the library at least twice a week since she quit. When the staff had asked after Elspeth, Ursula told them this was her place of sanctuary. Somewhere she could escape from her mother, if only for an hour.

Retirement at sixty-five wasn't compulsory in more enlightened times, and Ursula continued to patrol the bookshelves of her beloved library until she reached seventy-five. She often remarked that she would have done the job for nothing.

Times had changed. Ursula realised that the people who visited the library were nowhere near as well-behaved as those she remembered from her earlier years.

"There are signs everywhere," she would say. "Why do they bother coming here if they can't read? Quiet means just that. Either don't talk or whisper. I've lost count of the number of times I've had to reprimand people. As for the unemployed, or the retirees, they wander indoors for warmth and to read the daily newspaper. They can't afford to buy one because they need every penny in their pocket when the pubs open. I needn't look at the clock on the wall. I know when it's eleven o'clock because there's a queue at the door to get out. It's worse in the afternoons. They troop back in, smelling of drink, and often something far worse."

When Ursula retired, she didn't stop visiting the library. She still popped in whenever she was in town. Old habits are hard to break. Noisy schoolchildren and drunken senior citizens with flatulence continued to feel the sharp edge of her tongue.

Ursula was an avid reader, and the things that occupied her mind while she sat in silence poring over her work wouldn't have been what most observers would expect.

Wednesday, 16 January 2013

AS SHE RELAXED in her father's chair by the fireside, Ursula let her mind drift back over the benefits of living alone.

There was a special magic in sitting in the kitchen in the morning, reading or waiting for the bread to bake. She could lounge on the sofa, checking the headlines on the daily newspaper in the middle of the afternoon if she wished. Knick-knacks surrounded her on an evening such as this. Items that had belonged to her parents or that Ursula collected on recent holidays abroad.

Ursula knew with absolute certainty that no one could tell her she had too many books, several unnecessary scatter cushions, and that the television was far too loud. Why? Because she lived alone and she loved it. The trick had been to arrange her life the way she wanted it after her mother died.

"I don't see any biological reason women should marry or have children," she'd told Glenda, her sister-in-law, last weekend. "I was reading an article in the library just this week that suggested men and women were never meant to stay together for a long time. They should procreate and leave. No wonder so many modern marriages fail. Once any children can survive alone, there's no point continuing the relationship. Look at you and Arthur. You've spent the last thirty years hating the sight of one another. Where are you off tomorrow? Visiting your son, I suppose? Matthew's fifty-seven, married, with two children and three grandchildren. He doesn't need you. What did you do after you fell pregnant with him? You stopped working and became a full-time housewife. You loved that job and could have gone on to higher positions at that bank. If a young woman today wants to focus on a career, it's simpler to remain single. Look at your Samantha. You never see her from one Christmas to the next. She's flying around the world on long-haul flights as an air stewardess. Samantha was sensible enough to realise she didn't need a man to validate her existence."

Glenda gave the same response as everyone else of her generation. It's what you did back then.

Being single all these years had given Ursula valuable time to pursue her pet projects and be her own person. She was happy she'd used her time alone to figure out who she was.

Ursula turned the volume up another notch on the TV. Her neighbours were one hundred yards in either direction; they wouldn't hear. It's odd how these things creep up on you as you get older. She could spot a loud whisper in the library when she returned to work after her mother passed.

The year before she retired, Ursula noticed subtle changes in her hearing. Colleagues would nudge her arm to catch her attention. She would apologise and claim she was engrossed in an article or the blurb of a new book and hadn't heard them speak. Then, a year later, she watched her colleagues' lips to confirm what she thought they were saying. In the past three years, things had gotten worse.

Because the bungalow stood on a quiet road, surrounded by trees on three sides, Ursula no longer followed her parents' custom of drawing every curtain in the house the minute the sun set. Why bother? There was never anyone in the open fields beyond the trees after sundown. The occasional car passed the bungalow on winter evenings, but nobody came calling.

Ursula enjoyed seeing the moon and stars through her bedroom window when she went to bed and the sun when it woke her in the mornings. It was another mechanism she had adopted to celebrate her single life. If she undressed in the dark before slipping into bed or wandered naked to the bathroom in the morning, who's business was it but her own?

Ursula had established a strict rota for visitors that matched her daily calendar. Don Hillier arrived on Tuesday and Thursday at ten o'clock. Don was ten years younger than Ursula and hadn't adjusted to retirement. He needed to keep busy. Ursula paid him to tend to the garden and those annoying little jobs that an ageing property accumulates.

Don had been her handyman for three years but had never once stepped inside the bungalow. His employment was strictly for outdoor maintenance. He offered to fix a dripping tap or move heavy furniture to let Ursula spring-clean the place. All offers received a polite but firm refusal. Ursula insisted she could manage what needed doing. Don held his tongue. Everything stayed as it had been when he arrived to mow the lawn for the first time.

Ursula visited the library on Monday, Wednesday, and Friday morning. Saturday was the one day in the week when she spent more than the minimum amount of time away from the bungalow. Her first job in the morning was to get her baking done for the coming week. Then she went into town to do her weekly shop at the supermarket. She was strict about delivery time. After shopping, she had lunch at the corner café before spending two hours in her beloved library. She arrived home at four fifteen precisely to await the supermarket delivery van at half-past four.

One might have expected Ursula to treat Sundays differently from her parents. But, instead, she attended the Mere Methodist Church services at ten-thirty and seven o'clock in the evening.

On this particular Wednesday evening, Ursula sat closer to the roaring log fire. Don Hillier had sawn plenty of wood to keep her warm during this cold snap, but the outside temperature hadn't risen above freezing all day. The trip to town to visit the library had been an adventure. Almost every step she'd taken on the pavements risked a fall. At seventy-eight, Ursula knew how dangerous that could prove.

She was thankful to be safe indoors and could no longer hear the wind rattling the loose guttering Don was due to fix tomorrow. She glanced at the television. How long had it been since the programme she'd been watching had finished? Her mind had wandered. Was there anything worth staying up to watch? Ursula turned off the TV, got up from her chair and went into the kitchen. It was time for a cup of hot chocolate to take across the hallway to her bedroom. Then, standing at the sink to fill the kettle, she saw something move in the back garden.

Was that someone standing under the apple tree in the far corner? She couldn't make out a face from this distance. What did they think they were doing? Ursula hesitated. Was it her imagination? The trees were twenty yards away, and the movement had ceased. It must have been a trick of the moonlight. The kettle soon boiled, and Ursula carried the cup in both hands back into the living room.

The cup of hot chocolate hit the floor, and Ursula screamed. There was a face at the front window. The image was familiar. The person wore one of those Scream masks that were everywhere at Halloween. A second later, the face disappeared. Ursula scurried to the window as best she could. It must be children, she thought. The little devils wanted to scare her. Well, perhaps it was time to draw the curtains after all.

As she stretched to draw the curtains together, the masked face sprang up from beneath the window. Ursula screamed again and staggered backwards.

She cursed the silence.

Ursula hadn't closed the curtains completely. She stared at the gap, praying the person had run away. Maybe they were next door now, terrorising her neighbour, Beryl Giddings. This silly game had gone on long enough. She should call the police.

A shape darted past the window, heading for her front door.

The landline was in the hallway. Ursula moved towards the door.

She hadn't heard the back door opening. All she could

think about was the person wearing the Scream mask staring at her through the gap in the curtain.

Something alerted Ursula to the danger behind her. Unfortunately, she turned too late as she felt a crushing blow to the back of her head and fell to the floor.

Ursula Wakeley didn't see the person behind her run to the door to let in their accomplice. Her attackers studied the huddled shape on the floor. The old witch was still breathing. Okay, now it was time to have fun.

Chapter Two

Thursday, 17 January 2013

DON HILLIER PUSHED his bicycle along Shaftesbury Road at the appointed time. He passed the gateway to Two Counties Farm as he gingerly made his way towards Ursula Wakeley's bungalow.

He thought it odd that Ursula hadn't drawn her curtains at this time of day.

Don had set off from home earlier than usual. The gritters were out last night, and the major roads were passable for traffic. Once you ventured onto the side streets and lanes, however, then you were asking for trouble. Don felt safer with his bicycle to lean on as he slipped and skated the last part of his journey. There was a weak sun this morning. However, the forecast was improving, and the temperature was in the low digits.

He expected to see Ursula at the front door, ready to issue new instructions, but there was no sign. He rested his bicycle against the front porch, stepped up and rang the doorbell. She couldn't have gone into town, could she? It was Thursday.

Don decided to get on with repairing the guttering. He walked to the garden shed at the side of the bungalow and carried the short ladder to the front. He rested it against the top row of bricks, and after checking the foot of the ladder was secure, he climbed.

The gap in the curtains didn't allow the handyman to see much of the living room. Two things looked strange to Don. When did he last see these curtains drawn, anyway? He couldn't recall, and there was a stain on the carpet by the kitchen door. He didn't believe Ursula would leave it that way for so long. As his eyes grew accustomed to the dark interior of the house, he saw that the back door was open.

Ursula was nowhere to be seen in the back garden when he fetched the ladder from the shed. He would have heard her. There was something amiss. Don didn't possess a mobile phone, so he walked to Charles Marshall's next door. He knew the older man was up, as he'd seen Charles putting something in the recycling bin when he came along the road. It was probably another empty gin bottle.

He tapped on the front door.

"Don, what can I do for you?" asked Charles.

"Ursula isn't answering her door, Charles. The back door's open. I'm afraid something might have happened to her."

"Do you want me to ring for an ambulance? Maybe Ursula went outside in the dark last night and slipped on the ice?"

Don knew Ursula's reaction if they made a mountain out of a molehill.

"Do you have her brother Arthur's number?" asked Don.

"It'll be in the directory. Let me give Arthur a call. Come on in out of the cold, Don."

Ten minutes later, Arthur Wakeley drove past the Marshall residence and swung into the driveway of his sister's bungalow. It was clear to Don Hillier that Arthur was not best pleased.

"I'll get along there and explain," said Don, "many thanks for your help, Charles."

"No problem. Let me know, won't you? She can be a funny old stick but a good neighbour."

"You mean she never bothers you," laughed Don.

"Ha, exactly," said Charles.

When Don reached the entrance to the driveway, Arthur was already inside the bungalow. Don wasn't surprised that Arthur had a key. He stood outside on the porch and waited.

Arthur reappeared.

"You're as white as a sheet, Arthur," said Don. "Is everything alright?"

"I need to phone the police," said Arthur, "someone broke in last night and…."

"Not dead," said Don, "surely you can't mean someone killed Ursula?"

Arthur shook his head.

"I can't go back in there," he said, "what he did to her. He must be an animal."

LOCAL NEWSPAPERS CARRIED various reports of the spinster's murder throughout the police investigation.

'Miss Ursula Wakeley was seventy-eight years old when

someone stabbed her to death in her bungalow on Shaftesbury Road, Mere. Her elder brother Arthur found the body. Don Hillier, a handyman expecting to work for the retired librarian, raised the alarm.'

'Ursula Wakeley's death prompted the largest police investigation in the town's history, and, despite the attraction of a sizeable reward, they never identified her killer. Police believed the killer lived in the local area and was shielded by a friend or family member after the murder.'

'The killer broke into the rear of her home to rob Miss Wakeley and repeatedly stabbed her when she challenged him. The killer removed a quantity of jewellery from one bedroom. Police estimated the value of the haul at only two thousand pounds.'

Wednesday, 27 June 2018 - Devizes

NEIL KNEW what an idiot he had been. When Gus asked him to hang around for a chat about his trip to Gablecross the other morning, he suspected that it was a smokescreen. Gus knew him well enough by now to know he could handle a fact-finding mission with work colleagues alone.

No, it had to be Amelia. She was a handful, and no mistake.

Nothing happened after they got into the taxi to make the driver blush, and Neil got Amelia out onto the pavement as soon as possible when they reached her place. Her hands were everywhere, urging him to stay, but he insisted he needed to continue the taxi journey home. Yes, she'd rung him at silly o'clock to explain what he could do to her in detail. But there was no excuse for her calling Melody the next day, asking her to thank him for a splendid night. That was just vindictive.

Neil hadn't found that out until after he left the office and drove to London Road. He intercepted Amelia Cranston on her way to the car park and told her nothing could be between them. He was married and wanted to stay married. Amelia didn't waste a second before telling Neil what she'd done.

"Why on earth did you do that?" he'd asked.

"I want you, Neil," she whined, "and you wanted me too. You can't deny it."

"Whether or not I found you attractive is irrelevant," he'd said. "I'm not available, and that's that."

"You'll regret it," said Amelia.

Neil had left her standing in the middle of the car park. He didn't look back.

After Gus gave them the surprise holiday, Neil drove home, and his first call was to Melody at her mother's house.

"Hi, Melody. Please tell me you're ready to come home. I miss you."

"Did you go out with the gang on Friday night, Neil?" asked Melody.

"We went to the Waggon & Horses," said Neil. "Gus had delivered the goods yet again on a case. It was a good night. Even Alex Hardy made it."

"That silly cow Amelia called me on Saturday morning. I don't think she'd sobered up yet, because she asked me to thank you for a good night."

"She invited herself to our night out," said Neil. "Amelia worked with me on my Dad's case, and she filled in for a day or two when Suzie Ferris was missing. I don't think she'll ever get a permanent slot on the team. Gus wasn't that keen to see her there."

"Did you share a taxi or something?"

"Yeah, it made sense. No way was I going out on a Friday night without having a drink. You know me."

"All too well," said Melody. "My Mum's had enough of me. She keeps asking when I'm going home. I needed her for the first few weeks after we lost the baby, but now I need to be with you."

"We can make it work once we're back together under the same roof, Melody," said Neil.

"We can," said Melody, "what time will you be over to collect me?"

"I'm leaving now," said Neil.

Neil had collected Melody from her mother's, and they returned home.

"I can't believe this," said Melody as she stepped through the front door.

"What?" asked Neil.

"I expected to find you'd been living in a tip for the past few weeks. When did you tidy up the place? Just before you rang?"

"The house seemed so empty," said Neil. "I tidied the nursery, so it didn't add to the pain when you felt ready to come home. Once I started on that, it made sense to keep on top of the rest of the house. It gave me something to occupy my mind."

"Mum helped keep me occupied, too; she didn't want me sitting and thinking of what we'd lost. We can help each other now. I spoke to the doctor on Monday. There's no reason we can't try again when we're ready."

"What do you want to do next?" asked Neil.

"Let's go up to the nursery together," said Melody. "I've

got to face it before I can move on. Once I've cleared that hurdle, we can spend the rest of your break making up for our time apart. You know what they say: if it isn't broke, don't fix it. We were fine before the miscarriage. We'll be fine in the future."

As they stood in the small bedroom they'd decorated ready for their first-born child, Neil knew Melody was right. They had been happy, and losing the little one was a terrible wrench. There was no reason things couldn't get back to how they were.

Neil hoped that Amelia Cranston's last comment was an empty threat.

Wednesday, 27 June 2018 - Warminster

LUKE SHERMAN and Nicky spent the first morning of their break wondering what to do with their unexpected free time. Luke wanted to jump in the car and head for the coast. Many places would be fully booked, but somewhere was always available in one of the quieter seaside towns.

As lunchtime approached, Nicky complained that they risked wasting a day. Rather than have a long weekend by the coast, they should do something about the house.

Luke looked around the lounge-diner and the kitchen.

"I suppose you're right," he reluctantly agreed. "We couldn't afford to change everything to suit our taste when we moved here. We concentrated on the bedrooms and the bathroom and then stopped."

"We've got lazy," said Nicky. "There's nothing wrong with our furniture and the bits and pieces we've added. The walls, ceilings, and doors look tired. Everything needs a coat of paint."

"Agreed," said Luke, "it's high time the ground-floor rooms got the treatment.

Five minutes later, they were visiting their local DIY store to buy wallpaper, paint, and tools that their parents had let them borrow in the past.

As they stood at the checkout with a pasting table, brushes, a set of screwdrivers, twelve rolls of wallpaper, and six cans of paint, Luke nudged Nicky's arm.

"Will you marry me?" he asked.

"Why now?" asked Nicky.

"Who else does this," said Luke, pointing at the over-flowing trolley, "except an old married couple?"

"I suppose you're right," said Nicky, "in that case, it's a yes."

They had been together for years without needing to make things official. So they drove home, emptied the car, decided which room to decorate first, and went back into Warminster looking for rings.

Luke and Nicky didn't arrive home until the early hours - any excuse for a celebratory meal and far too many drinks.

"We need to get up and start on the lounge," said Nicky. "It's Thursday already, and it's gone eight."

"I need a shower and breakfast before I can think of stripping off that old wallpaper," said Luke. "Wouldn't it be better to pop into town to pick up travel brochures? Last night we couldn't decide between the Caribbean or the Maldives for our honeymoon."

Nicky groaned.

"You're incorrigible,"

"Don't blame me," said Luke, "you should have turned

me down. So which is it to be? The Maldives or the Caribbean?"

"The lounge first," said Nicky, "and we'll spin a coin tonight after we've done a day's work."

"Roll on Monday when I get back to work," said Luke.

Wednesday, 27 June 2018 - Urchfont and Devizes

GUS FREEMAN WAS up with the lark.

Not because he was in a rush to get anywhere. He had sat in the lounge last night, going over the previous week's events. The Burnside case had left him with more questions than answers. No matter how he tried to analyse it, he kept coming up against a brick wall.

Times like these left him unable to sleep. Grant Burnside's case kept gnawing away at him and made him question whether he should still try to do this job.

After an hour of lying awake listening to bird-song, Gus decided enough was enough. A shower, followed by a hearty breakfast, was required. There was a slight irritation of a trip to London Road to suffer, and then he was free for the day.

Suzie was working. Everything was in place for tonight's get-together with Bert Penman and his family. Bert's daughter, Margaret Hadlee, was coming to the village with her nephew, Brett Penman.

The Canadian veterinary physician was driving Margaret from the Colerne hotel where they were staying. Gus had no idea which of the local places of interest the couple might visit today. He would hear it from Bert's daughter tonight.

If he could spend the least time with the ACC, then a good four hours on the allotment wasn't out of the question. He was his own boss for a change, and he could put the afternoon to good use. Not only catching up with long-delayed chores but having another crack at unravelling the Grant Burnside mystery.

The shower refreshed him, and the cooked breakfast satisfied the inner man. As soon as he stepped outside the bungalow and felt the warmth of the summer sun, he strode towards the Focus with renewed purpose. It felt good to be alive on days such as this.

Gus eased his car into the steady stream of traffic on the A342 as it snaked its way through the Lydeway and onwards to the bustling market town. Twelve minutes later, Gus was on London Road. Surely, this was too good to last? He turned into the Police HQ entrance and searched for a vacant spot in the Visitor's car park. He was in luck.

As he got out of the car, he glanced at the ACC's office window. Should he give Kenneth Truelove, the Acting Chief Constable, a wave? As usual, it was difficult to tell whether his leader was in a good mood. Rather than risk an altercation on such a pleasant morning, Gus lowered his gaze and headed for the front door.

"Good morning, Mr Freeman," said the desk sergeant.

Things had changed somewhat since that first visit at the end of March.

Who would have believed the new team the ACC asked him to join had achieved so much in twelve weeks? After signing in, Gus climbed the stairs to the first floor and scanned the administration area for friendly faces.

"Come on, Freeman," snapped Kenneth Truelove. "I haven't got all day to watch you daydreaming."

The ACC stood in the doorway of his office. Gus

noticed that the dress uniform he'd mentioned last week was getting an outing, and there was no denying it. The ACC was carrying excess timber.

Gus sensed Vera Butler and Kassie Trotter hovering for a quick chat before he disappeared behind the ACC's door. They might have briefed him on balloons flying out of control in the vicinity if he'd left home a minute earlier.

Geoff Mercer came scuttling along the dark corridor that led to his office. He looked out of breath. What the heck had happened since yesterday? Everyone seemed to be in a rush at HQ this morning. Gus wasn't as concerned about what was getting the ACC het up as how it might influence the time he remained here. He had places to go, vegetables to harvest, and a visit to town for a haircut. Ah, well, let's get it over with.

Geoff Mercer didn't offer Gus any insight as he went into the office ahead of him. The ACC had already sat at his desk, which was never a good sign.

"Did you receive a call from Gareth Francis yesterday, Freeman?" asked the ACC.

"He called to thank me for solving several crimes his new colleagues at Gablecross should have sorted," said Gus, "nothing out of the ordinary. He mentioned that Vic Hodge and Kerry Burnside were ready to co-operate. I think he said that Vic was singing like a bird. Why, what's the problem?"

"Gareth thought you ended the call abruptly. He is considering an official complaint."

"I blame the modern approach, Sir," said Gus, "this sensitivity training that officers receive these days isn't doing you any favours. DI Francis said he was looking forward to working with me again. I thought you moved him twenty miles up the road, so I never needed to work with him again. He's not the worst detective I've encountered, but he ranks in the top three."

"I calmed him, Gus," said Geoff Mercer. "I think you'll escape censure on this occasion. You do have to watch what you say to people these days. Every word can be open to interpretation."

"Did he get the right answers from Kerry Burnside?" asked Gus.

"It was a disaster," said the ACC. "Patrick Iverson suddenly appeared at her office when Gareth and DS Latimer were due to conduct the interview. Ms Burnside switched from giving them chapter and verse to a series of no comments."

"I begged Gareth to take it easy with her. She struck me as someone who would clam up if he treated her as being in the same bracket as her brother, Gary. Kerry wasn't even as involved in the darker side of the business as Henry and Joseph, let alone the stuff Gary carried out. Kerry received no love or kindness throughout her life from any male family member. Suzie Ferris could have gotten her to give us so much more. So what's happening now?"

"Iverson is pinning his hopes on discrediting Hodge's statement," said Kenneth Truelove. "Iverson told Gareth Francis that Hodge would say anything to get his sentence reduced."

"Did Gablecross take Henry and Joseph in for questioning?" asked Gus.

"They waited until they had completed the interviews with Hodge and Kerry Burnside," said the ACC.

"So that pair have had another twenty-four hours to get rid of the evidence," said Geoff Mercer.

"There's one saving grace," said Gus. "Gary's dead, and Hodge and Drewett aren't in town to do another clean-up job. Henry and Joseph don't have the stomach for that. There are still other witnesses we could turn."

"What do you mean, we?" asked the ACC. "you handed everything your team gathered over to Gablecross. It's not your job to see the case through to the bitter end."

"I meant London Road, Sir," said Gus, "I know it won't be popular, but get the case back and let Geoff oversee it here at Devizes. Use Suzie Ferris and another female detective to persuade Kerry Burnside there's a way that she and Vic Hodge can come out of this with only a few scratches. We know Kerry contacted Gina Burnside and encouraged her to let what remains of the Burnside family help get her on her feet. One way or another, Henry and Joseph's drug ring has to get shut down. We can't allow Iverson to end his career on another win for the Burnside gang."

"You're right," said the ACC, "it would be unpopular. So I'll send DI Ferris to Gablecross to work alongside DI Francis for a month. Her task will be to do as you suggest. Explore every avenue to help Gareth end the Burnside gang's grip on the town. If Vic Hodge and Kerry Burnside get off with a slap on the wrist, so be it. The bigger picture is what counts. We can rely on DI Ferris to convince Gareth Francis it was his idea."

Geoff Mercer and Gus Freeman shared a look. In a month, they could guarantee that the whole idea would have been the ACC's if Suzie had delivered the goods. Another feather in Kenneth's cap justified the PCC's decision to ask him to step into the breach as Acting Chief Constable.

Gus wasn't worried about who took the credit as long as they got the desired result.

He hoped that Kenneth Truelove realised that his chances of being offered the Chief Constable's role full-time would improve dramatically if Gus's suggestion did the trick.

The ACC had stood up and returned to the window. Gus wondered whether he saw any balloons in the sky. Was that all that got him so het up earlier?

"Do you have anything new for me, Sir?" asked Gus, eager to get on with his day.

"It's too soon to discuss that," said the ACC, returning to his desk. "Mercer talked me through this Grant Burnside business yesterday, and guess what? I had a call later in the afternoon from Jack Sanders. I haven't spoken to the fellow in five years and couldn't understand why a retired DCI rang me. Sanders told me he had a lengthy conversation with you, Freeman, but he was disappointed that you didn't appreciate the obvious connection between the events he described."

"I couldn't follow the logic, Sir," said Gus. "I spent a large part of yesterday evening at home trying to make the pieces fit for Grant Burnside's murder. Colonel Sanders told me a tale about a girl called Tanya Norris, who disappeared several years ago. Four dodgy individuals, who Jack asserted were exploiting two dozen teenage girls, followed her in quick order. I'm at a loss to explain how that connected with our red-headed sniper from Cheney Manor."

"What about Mercer's point concerning the inter-gang warfare at the turn of the century? Surely, that must have piqued your interest?"

"Geoff told me of that affair before I started work here," said Gus. "It's far easier to believe that four members of one gang got taken out, and then their colleagues responded with four thugs from the gang they blamed. Geoff mentioned a doctor who got tied up in that business too. Perhaps he was in the wrong place at the wrong time.

The doctor wasn't as white as snow. He was selling drugs to the gang leader when their rivals took revenge. My immediate reaction was that it was a tit-for-tat affair, rather than someone highlighting to the police in a very bloody way that they weren't doing their job."

"Is that how you view the Swindon situation then, Gus?" asked Geoff Mercer.

"That's not so easy to explain," said Gus. "I'd want to know where Tanya Norris went after she left the hospital. Who collected her, and why was Tanya willing to go with them? According to Jack Sanders, she hadn't been able to trust anyone for the previous two years. Her sole purpose in life, working for these four men, was to service dozens of Muslim men every day of the week. Several years have passed since, but where is Tanya Norris today?"

"Where do we look for her?" asked Geoff Mercer.

"Social media," said Gus, "if there are any photographs of her online, the Hub whizz-kids should find them. Tanya's parents came from Oxford; they must have pictures of her before she ran away from home at twelve. Get the experts to age those photos and start the hunt. If she's alive, then Tanya will be out there somewhere."

"Who drove that Porsche?" asked the ACC. "The one that raced out towards Shrivenham or wherever. Those brothers in the BMW disappeared, and the car was a burned-out wreck before daybreak."

"The two events aren't necessarily connected," said Gus. "Half a dozen burn-ups occur on dual-carriageways and bypasses across the county every night. We've got unmarked high-performance cars parked on the side of the M4, with officers doing nothing more than watching for cars travelling over the limit. The Porsche and the BMW raced for a while and then went their separate ways. Jack Sanders never mentioned CCTV evidence placing them on the same road together after the first time they appeared on camera at those traffic lights. Maybe the brothers crashed the car later that night and trashed it. Were both brothers banned at the time? Have they ever taken a driving test in this country? Tax. Insurance. Was that BMW stolen? Was it being driven under the influence of alcohol, drugs, or both? There are plenty of reasons to explain those things we know happened. Why hasn't anyone seen those four men since? Now that's a different matter, but who's to say they didn't move to Bradford or return to Pakistan? Jack Sanders believes someone killed them because they were allegedly responsible for the worst sexual exploitation. Where's the evidence of that? Why wasn't Gablecross aware of what was happening on their patch? Don't tell me. Social Services knew girls had gone missing from care homes, but they didn't want to rock the boat."

"I need to make it my business to find out why that gang never got hauled in," said the ACC. "So, you think Jack Sanders's idea was fanciful, Freeman, is that it? You don't believe there's a sinister hand at work."

"I don't dismiss it entirely, Sir," said Gus. "We need more information first. If we trace Tanya Norris, she could give us more names. At least twenty young girls had disappeared when the BMW stopped smouldering. I'd want to talk to several of those girls."

"Which leads us back to Grant Burnside," said Geoff Mercer.

Gus spotted a glance between the two men on the other side of the desk.

"Okay, if you've got something to say, say it," said Gus.

"The Crime Review Team didn't use the Hub resource much on the last two cases you tackled," said Kenneth

Truelove. "I stressed its importance when you returned to work. Next Monday, you will have three Detective Sergeants at your disposal, plus the two ladies. I propose that DS Hardy works here at London Road in the Hub."

"What's the aim of that secondment, and how long would it last?" asked Gus.

"His task would be to find the red-headed sniper," said Geoff Mercer. "It will take as long as it takes."

"Alex is good, as you well know," said Gus. "I could have him back by Tuesday."

"Something lies hidden behind what happened in 2002 and the events in Swindon," said Geoff Mercer. "If Alex identifies Grant Burnside's killer, then the ACC and I wish to question that man on every suspicious death reported in the interim. First, we want to know whether he acted alone."

"You're determined to pursue this theory that there's a group of vigilante killers out there that nobody has spotted. Not just Wiltshire Police but every force across the country. Next, you'll call Brendan Curran and get the Organised Crime Task Force to help you take down these people."

"It crossed my mind," said the ACC.

Gus was going to say they should let this hypothetical vigilante group get on with it. If they took out two dozen hardened criminals, it was two dozen less for the police to handle. He was saved from an ear-bashing from the ACC by a knock on the door.

It was coffee-time, and Kassie Trotter entered the room with her trolley.

Chapter Three

"AH, YOU'RE A LIFESAVER, KASSIE," said Gus as she handed him his coffee.

"Well, I've got the buoyancy tanks, Mr Freeman," she replied.

"Have you forgotten what I said about watching every word you say?" Geoff asked Gus.

Gus was going to protest his innocence when the ACC chipped in.

"I've got a spare tyre, Kassie," he said. "You can see what your buns are doing to my dress uniform. I struggled to get the buttons done up this morning."

"Just as well that I made another Madeira cake then," said Kassie. "Vera will wheel my cakes through the door in a tick."

Kassie saw the sad face that Geoff Mercer had adopted.

"Don't worry, Mr Mercer," she said. "I can offer you something more substantial. I know you're partial to a Chelsea bun."

"So am I," groaned the ACC.

Vera arrived in the doorway. Gus thought her hair looked shorter. It suited her and made her look ten years younger.

"A slice of Madeira for me, please, Vera," he said. "I don't want to spoil my appetite for tonight."

"Another night out?" asked Vera with a smile. "You're never home."

"I'm dining with friends," Gus replied. "Bert Penman's daughter and grandson are in the country for a few more days. We're eating at the Lamb."

"Vera will think of you while she's home alone with a packet of crisps," said Kassie as she breezed past Gus with her trolley and headed for the door.

When the door had closed behind them, Kenneth Truelove sighed.

"A packet of crisps. I can't remember when my wife last let me have one crisp, let alone a packet."

"I've heard that exercise is good for you, Sir," said Gus.

"Retirement would be better," said the ACC. "Now, where did we get to?"

"You wanted me to agree to lose DS Hardy for an indefinite period the minute he returns to work, Sir."

"Well?" asked the ACC.

"No problem, Sir," said Gus, "but what about DI Ferris? Will she work normal office hours while she prevents Gareth Francis from becoming a liability? We can't afford him to foul up chances of convictions in the Burnside case."

"That sounds reasonable," said Geoff Mercer, "do you agree, Sir?"

Kenneth Truelove nodded and walked to the window. Regular service could be resumed.

"Where are we off to for our next cold case then, Sir?" asked Gus.

Geoff Mercer shook his head, trying to stop Gus.

Gus realised it might have been him that let go of that balloon he was concerned over earlier. Was it one of his old cases that the ACC wanted to review? That could be awkward.

"Do you remember the Wakeley case, Freeman?" asked the ACC. He didn't move from the window.

"I worked in Salisbury at the time, Sir. It affected everyone. It was a nasty business."

"Who ran the investigation?" asked the ACC.

"DCI Melvin Jefferson was the Senior Investigating Officer," said Gus. "I was due to be on the team with him. We worked together on dozens of cases. Mel asked me to take charge of investigating a series of armed robberies. That was the case with the three villains I watched go to prison for the maximum term at Crown Court the day Tess died. I had worked on that caper for months, so I missed the Ursula Wakeley investigation."

"Are you happy to review a case your friend and colleague handled?" asked the ACC.

"Of course, Sir," said Gus. "I came back to solve cold cases. I won't cherry-pick. The Mel Jefferson that I knew would have run a tight ship."

"Who took your place on the team?" asked Geoff Mercer.

"DI Fabian Kite," said Gus.

"Was that his actual name?" asked the ACC.

"His mother was a big fan of the singer Fabian, Sir," said Gus. "If Elvis hadn't arrived on the scene, Fabian Forte might have been a bigger star for longer. Hollywood came calling, and he made several films as well as having half a dozen hits in the Billboard Top 100 at the same time."

"No doubt you're right, Freeman," said Kenneth

Truelove. "Your musical knowledge is greater than mine. I thought they named him after Robert Fabian."

"Fabian of the Yard, you mean," said Geoff Mercer. "My parents watched that programme. It was one of the first CID shows on British television. Your colleagues must have given DI Kite a torrid time, Gus."

"Not because of the pop singer or the cop show. Fabian Kite was young, handsome, and a Freemason. He had everything going for him except a nose for solving crimes. After two years on the detective squad, Mel Jefferson suggested moving sideways into an office job. I believe he went into Human Resources."

"The murder occurred five years ago now," said the ACC, returning to his desk. "I'll refresh your memory on the basics."

"The crime scene photos were chilling from what I recall," said Gus. "When I was knee-deep in paperwork relating to that string of robberies, I didn't get the chance to do much more than glance at the whiteboards in the squad room. It always felt over-the-top for a mere break-in."

"The murder occurred on Wednesday the sixteenth of January in 2013," said Kenneth Truelove. "Ursula Wakeley, a seventy-eight-year-old spinster, got stabbed at her remote bungalow near Mere, Wiltshire. Ms Wakeley had lived in her parents' home all her life. The three-bedroomed bungalow stands on Shaftesbury Road several hundred yards from the Two Counties Farm, now a popular camping and caravanning site."

"Not that it was busy at that time of the year," said Gus. "I remember the south of the country suffering a severe cold snap that January. So most folks got wrapped up warm and indoors by five in the afternoon at the latest. So what time did the attack take place?"

"The police surgeon estimated the time of death between ten o'clock and midnight," said the ACC.

"Who discovered the body?" asked Gus.

"Ursula Wakeley used a handyman to carry out her gardening and house maintenance tasks," said Geoff Mercer. "Don Hillier, sixty-eight, arrived at ten o'clock on Thursday morning."

"Was he due to arrive that morning?" asked Gus.

"Yes, he worked Tuesday and Thursday every week for several years," said the ACC.

"Hillier was the first suspect Kite and Jefferson had in the frame," said Geoff, "they interviewed him frequently. Ms Wakeley was a stickler for time-keeping. She wouldn't accept a foot of snow as an excuse for Hillier arriving late, let alone patches of black ice on the roads and pavements. If she gave Don Hillier a list of jobs to complete, she expected them to get done before he finished for the day."

"I'm surprised he stayed so long," said Gus.

"DCI Jefferson asked why he didn't pack it in," said the ACC. "Hillier shrugged his shoulders and said he needed to keep busy. And it was just her way. She was a spinster, and Hillier reckoned they were odd creatures. DI Kite pressed Hillier on the number of times he'd been inside the bungalow. Forensics couldn't find any trace of him indoors. Kite couldn't believe Hillier had worked there for up to twelve hours a week for three years and never stepped inside the back door just for a cup of tea. What about using the toilet? Surely, there had to be occasions when nature called?"

"Hillier said Ursula insisted he brought a flask from home if he needed a drink," said Geoff. "Hillier cycled to the bungalow, so if he needed the loo, he cycled home. His house was only a ten-minutes ride towards town."

"I suppose she insisted he made up the lost time?" said Gus.

"Exactly," said Geoff.

"It surprised Hillier not to find his employer waiting for him, as you can imagine," said the ACC. "He didn't want to get in her bad books by loitering, so he fetched a ladder from the garden shed and repaired the guttering at the front of the bungalow. For some reason, Ms Wakeley never closed her curtains day or night. Perhaps when you live in the middle of nowhere, it doesn't seem important. Anyway, that morning they were part closed in the living room. Hillier climbed the ladder and noticed the door from the kitchen to the rear garden was open. Someone had smashed one of the glass panels."

"Why didn't he go inside?" asked Gus. "I know we never want the crime scene compromised, but most people would have gone into the house through the kitchen and called out her name. At seventy-eight, his employer could have fallen or been taken ill. My first reaction would be to check Ursula Wakeley didn't need medical assistance. No wonder the detectives thought Hillier a suspect. Instead of the natural reaction, it was as if he'd assumed the worst had happened."

"Well, maybe because Hillier didn't possess a mobile phone," said Geoff, "and because Ursula had never invited him in, he thought it best to run to a neighbour for help."

"The neighbouring properties belonged to Beryl Giddings, a widow, and Charles Marshall," said the ACC. "Charles was married to Gwen, and their house was the one Hillier visited. Marshall called Arthur Wakeley, Ursula's eighty-year-old brother. He drove across from the other side of Mere and let himself into the bungalow."

"Did Hillier tell him of the possible break-in at the rear of the property?" asked Gus.

"Marshall relayed the information Don Hillier gave him when he knocked on the door. Jefferson never questioned why Arthur had a set of keys to his family home. Why should he? Hillier sensed that Arthur was annoyed at getting the call. He left his wife at home, jumped in the car, and didn't offer Hillier a lift from the Marshalls' place. Arthur drove past and went inside the house before Don walked back along the road. Arthur's statement said that he looked into the living room and called out his sister's name. There was no response from the kitchen, so he went straight to the third bedroom."

"Ursula didn't sleep in her parents' bedroom then?" asked Gus.

"Arthur said his old room at the rear of the property was untouched since he left home to get married," said Geoff Mercer. "Ursula occupied the smaller room next to the family bathroom, and their parents, Gideon and Elspeth, slept in the main bedroom at the front. After her mother died in 1996, Ursula moved into the front bedroom. Arthur hadn't realised. They weren't close as a family. When Ursula socialised with Arthur and his wife, Glenda, it was always on neutral ground, such as a restaurant or a café."

"What did he find in her old bedroom?" asked Gus

"Nothing," said the ACC, "it was empty, except for half a dozen cardboard boxes filled with her parents' old clothes."

"So, he discovered the body in the main bedroom?" asked Gus.

"Ursula lay on the bed. Someone had scattered the

drawers from the dressing table on the floor nearby and discarded the empty jewellery boxes."

"I remember the crime scene photos," said Gus. "what did forensics determine?"

"Someone broke into the bungalow through the kitchen," said Geoff. "They used stone from a rockery to smash one of four squares of glass in the half-glazed door. No fingerprints were found at the scene, and the intruder wore gloves. They placed a thick cloth over the broken glass at the bottom of the pane and opened the door without cutting themselves."

"Old-style key or a Yale lock?" asked Gus.

"There was always a key left in the door, according to Arthur. When his parents were alive, they left it unlocked. The only things in the back fields were cows and stinging nettles."

"The killer left the cloth at the scene?" asked Gus.

"Yes, it came from designer jacketing fabric that retailed at thirty pounds per metre. There was nowhere in Mere that stocked the item."

"Interesting," said Gus. "What was the size of the pane of glass they broke?"

"Six inches square," said Geoff.

"Easier for a smaller hand, but not impossible for the likes of you or I," said Gus. "Especially if you took the trouble to knock out as much of the glass as possible."

"If the burglar entered the back garden from the fields surrounding the properties, they might have thought the place was empty," said the ACC.

"That was Jefferson's take on the murder, wasn't it?" asked Gus. "He thought Ursula disturbed a burglar looking for valuables, put up a fight, and suddenly, it became a murder."

"It made sense because a teenage girl took jewellery items into two second-hand shops in Ringwood at the week-end, looking for a quick sale." said the ACC.

"Ringwood is thirty miles away from Mere," said Gus. "How did they know there was a connection? Did Ursula have an insurance policy with photographs of her valuables? Did Arthur identify pieces he recalled his mother wore, perhaps?"

"According to Arthur, his mother never wore make-up or jewellery," said Geoff. "Gideon was a strict Methodist and didn't agree with vanities."

"Arthur's mother, Elspeth, died in 1996, and Ursula was no longer under her thumb," said the ACC. "Arthur told Jefferson that Ursula stayed home with her mother after Gideon died in a field behind the bungalow. That was way back in 1966. Imagine how tough that thirty years must have been for Ursula. To be trapped in that house with an ageing parent, unable to marry and have children. That could have made her very bitter. One thing she might have done as soon as she was free was to treat herself to a few vanities."

"So, nobody could confirm the items offered for sale in Ringwood came from the bungalow?" asked Gus.

"Fabian Kite took a statement from William Ormrod, the owner of one shop involved," said Geoff. "He described a bracelet, a necklace, and two cameo rings the girl had placed on the counter. Ormrod reckoned that the value of the four pieces was around two thousand pounds. He assumed the girl did not understand what she had there, so Ormrod offered the girl two hundred and fifty pounds. He counted out five fifty-pound notes on the counter, hoping she'd accept. She grabbed the notes and ran out of the shop. He saw her join a teenage boy wearing a hoodie waiting outside, and they disappeared."

"Could Ormrod give Fabian Kite a description of the girl?" asked Gus.

"Would you?" asked Geoff, "if you had conned her out of at least fifteen hundred quid? Ormrod didn't want to see her in his shop again. But, no, his description was vague. A winter coat. Knee-high brown leather boots, a scarf that covered half her face and long dark hair. He couldn't describe her features, eye colour, tattoos, or piercings. Kite asked about her hands. Did she wear rings? What was the state of her fingernails? Was there anything that might help identify her? Ormrod told him she wore gloves."

"Was there anyone else to ask whether those items belonged to Ursula Wakeley?" asked Gus.

"The staff at the library where she worked," said Geoff. "Ursula went there straight from school and stayed until her father died. Then she looked after her mother until 1996, as you heard. She resumed her old job, and according to Monica Butterworth, who has worked there for twenty-odd years, it was rare for Ursula to wear make-up or jewellery. Although she thought she remembered seeing Ursula with a cameo ring, it was inconclusive."

"I can't believe Jefferson didn't follow up on the nature of the break-in," said Gus.

"What do you mean?" asked the ACC.

"Well, what's the usual reason for someone breaking into a house? They want cash or something they can flog for with no questions asked. What will they do with the money? It's not going towards their next ski trip. It's heading for the pocket of their nearest drug dealer or putting food on the table. Was anything else stolen? Did the burglar search for Ursula's handbag, purse, or credit card? Forget what they did to the body for a moment. Did they rummage around in the other bedrooms to see whether any cash was hidden under a mattress? I don't buy that the only items they took away from the house were a handful of items from a dressing-table drawer."

Geoff Mercer was flicking through page after page of the murder file.

"Nothing else got taken, Gus," he said. "Ursula's handbag containing her purse, credit cards and keys lay on the floor by her chair. The purse held just over forty pounds in cash. Arthur confirmed that the only bedroom that looked as if anyone had been inside in years was where he found Ursula's body."

"What else do these burglars look for?" asked Gus.

"A mobile phone, tablet, or laptop," said the ACC, "anything portable."

"Ursula didn't possess any of those," said Geoff.

"They didn't look very hard for the cash, did they?" said Gus. "Why travel to Ringwood to sell the jewellery? Surely, there were loads of buyers within five miles of Mere. There's something else, too; time is of the essence in most break-ins. Most burglars want to get inside quickly. The burglar took longer than usual because of the precautions they took. They were eager not to leave fingerprints or blood, bringing the thick cloth piece along. I wonder why Ursula didn't hear the commotion."

"Beryl Giddings stated," said Geoff, "that Ursula's TV was loud enough to hear when she walked her dog past the bungalow in the evenings. That was until eighteen months before the murder. Beryl told Mel Jefferson that her Border Collie had died, and she never ventured out after dark."

"Did anyone at the library mention that Ursula was hard of hearing?" asked Gus.

"There's nothing in any of the statements, Gus," said Geoff. "Arthur and Glenda hadn't noticed. Don Hillier said if he stopped work for five minutes on a scorching afternoon, Ursula soon tapped on the window. He didn't think much was wrong with her hearing or eyesight."

"What did the other shop owner tell Kite?" asked Gus.

"He didn't see the young man," said Geoff, "it was just the girl who came into the shop. He asked her who the items belonged to and why she wanted to sell them."

"Did he do that, or was that what he thought Kite wanted to hear?" asked Gus.

"The girl got twitchy when questioned about the jewellery. Finally, the shop owner decided he didn't want to risk handling stolen goods. Kite noted that the shop owner thought she wasn't interested in the money; she just wanted to be rid of the jewellery."

"We keep coming back to the lack of confirmation that the two events are connected," said Gus. "Take that girl in Ringwood. It's possible a teenage girl smashed the window and opened the door, but do we believe she could be responsible for the murder?"

"Maybe there was an accomplice?" said Geoff.

"The hooded teenage male William Ormrod saw outside his shop," said the ACC.

"Time of death was said to be ten o'clock," said Gus. "Take me through the sequence, Geoff. Let's see if that makes more sense with the two people involved."

"The victim got struck from behind with a blunt object. Forensics found a clock garniture on the sideboard against the wall between the living room and the kitchen. The clock was flanked on either side by brass models of a shire horse set on an onyx base. Although the base of the nearest horse to the kitchen door had been wiped clean, they identified Ursula's DNA."

"So, the burglar whacked Ursula over the head with the first available heavy object," said the ACC.

"When you consider the planning that went into the break-in, it surprises me they didn't carry a weapon," said Gus.

"A single knife wound to the heart killed Ursula," said Geoff, reading from the file. "Blood loss would have been substantial. There was minimal blood spatter on the living room carpet."

"They moved Ursula from the living room to the bedroom while she was unconscious or still stunned from the initial blow," said the ACC. "Does that help us confirm that there were two attackers?"

"Ursula wasn't a big woman," said Geoff, "a healthy teenage boy or girl could drag her through to the bedroom alone."

"Was there a sexual motive to the break-in?" asked Gus.

"None," said Geoff. "Ursula was stripped naked and placed on the bed in a seated position. The fatal blow occurred somewhen between ten and midnight."

"Were they able to say whether Ursula regained consciousness?" asked Gus.

"The blow to the back of the head wouldn't have been enough to kill her. She was aware of what was going on within several minutes."

"What are we dealing with here?" asked Gus. "The autopsy indicated that everything else we can see on the crime scene photos happened post-mortem. The killer waited for Ursula Wakeley to regain consciousness before stabbing her. What does that suggest? They wanted her to know why she was about to die. What could a strait-laced, lonely spinster have possibly done to deserve such a fate? Where did they find the murder weapon?"

"In the kitchen drawer," said Geoff. "They had wiped it clean, the same as the garniture item, and put it back where they found it."

"Why didn't they leave as soon as they'd done the deed?" asked Gus. "Why did her killer continue to slash and mutilate Ursula's body for several hours? Only an animal does that."

"This wasn't about the break-in, was it?" said Geoff Mercer.

"Look, give me the murder file, and we'll get stuck into it on Monday. I don't want to jump to conclusions. I haven't seen everything Mel Jefferson and Fabian Kite saw surrounding this case. They marked it as a burglary that went wrong. The jewellery in Ringwood fitted that scenario. Several times on the Grant Burnside case, things popped up that I hadn't expected. When you rush to judgement, you can end up with egg on your face. We'll check that we've got every piece of the jigsaw before we put them together. I want to understand Ursula Wakeley better. Why was she a target? What made her stand out from the other single women in the area who lived alone?"

"You must work with fewer pieces than were available to Jefferson and Kite," said the ACC.

"At the time of the murder, her three neighbours were in their early eighties," said Geoff. "Beryl Giddings died in 2016. Charles Marshall is in a care home, as is his wife, Gwen. They're in separate homes because of the different amounts of nursing they require. So it's unlikely Charles could remember the statement he gave five years ago. Don Hillier and Monica Butterworth are the remaining reliable witnesses from Mere. Both shop owners are still trading if you wish to speak with them."

"Can we talk to Mel Jefferson and Fabian Kite?" asked Gus.

"Mel retired to South Africa last year," said Geoff.

"Oh yes, I remember his son worked for a bank in Jo'burg," said Gus.

"Fabian Kite left the force in 2016. Whereabouts unknown."

"We think he went into private security on mainland Europe," said the ACC. "If he wants to stay hidden, we might have trouble finding him. He was disillusioned with the job when he left. Fabian might stick two fingers at us if we ask him to co-operate with you on an old case."

"We'll see how far we get on our own," said Gus. "No need to panic just yet."

Chapter Four

GUS LEFT Kenneth Truelove and Geoff Mercer to their coffee and cake. He was already later than he had planned. The Ursula Wakeley murder file tucked under his arm promised to prove challenging. Too many people involved in 2013 had either died or could not answer the questions the case posed.

What was it Neil Davis said at times like this? Nobody said it was going to be easy, guv. That summed it up. As he took the stairs to the ground floor, he wondered how his colleague was getting on. With Alex Hardy off the case, Gus would need to have Neil firing on four cylinders until he ended his search for the red-headed mystery man.

Vera Butler came through the front door as he signed out at Reception.

"Have fun tonight," she said.

"You know how much I enjoy Bert Penman's company," said Gus. "I feel duty-bound to help him entertain his daughter and grandson."

"Margaret's the grandson's aunt, isn't she?" asked Vera,

"David was Brett's father. It's a long time since I saw either of Bert's children. I remember them at school. Of course, they were several years ahead of me, but I knew them by sight."

"That's right. Brett's in his mid-thirties, and you might see him around town soon. He plans to move back to the UK now his family is gone. Bert will have a lodger once Brett settles his affairs in Canada."

"If he needs a place to rent, Monty will have something, I'm sure," said Vera.

"The ACC told me our new Police Surgeon has already snapped up one of your ex-husband's properties. So there won't be much choice left for young Brett."

"Rhys Evans, yes," said Vera. "A rugged rugby-playing surgeon in his early thirties. He'll set a few hearts fluttering."

"I'm sure he will," said Gus. "I must dash; our leader kept me upstairs far longer than I hoped. I've got a busy day ahead before I let my hair down tonight."

"It's curling over your collar, Gus. It suits you."

"No, it has to go," said Gus. "A haircut is on the list of things to do before Suzie arrives at seven this evening."

"You're under orders then?" said Vera with a wicked grin. She left Gus by the door and bounced up the stairs to the first floor.

Gus returned to his car and threw the murder file on the passenger seat. A rugged rugby-playing surgeon. Was that what lay behind the shorter hairstyle? Kassie had competition.

Gus hesitated as he waited for a gap in traffic on London Road. Yes, getting the haircut out of the way made sense before returning to Urchfont. Otherwise, it wouldn't get done. So he reversed the Focus, returned to the parking space he had just left and walked into the town centre.

It was one o'clock when Gus reached the allotment. After he'd paid an excessive sum for a trim, he'd bought a gut-busting pasty from a well-known bakery chain to save making himself a sandwich. As a result, the murder file was now in the lounge of his bungalow, on ice until tomorrow evening.

The afternoon belonged to his fruit and vegetables. Gus opened his shed, retrieved the notes designed to keep him on the exact timetable as Bert Penman, and selected the correct tools. One glance at Bert's plot told him he was a week behind at best. It was time to get stuck in.

When nobody was around to chat with them or interrupt his train of thought, it was amazing how much progress he could make. Then, as the church clock drew in its breath to announce the arrival of six o'clock, Gus heard a familiar voice.

"Gus, I thought you would have gone by now? You're hot and sweaty. Have you forgotten about this evening?"

"Good evening, Reverend," said Gus, "I'll be clean and presentable by seven-thirty, don't you fret. Did you drop by to check on me?"

"Not at all," said Clemency, "I need to harvest my salad items. After allowing myself the odd indiscretion later tonight, it will be back to basic rations from tomorrow."

Gus studied the slimmer version of the Vicar of Dibley that stood before him. Clemency had tied her sun hat under her chin with a bow, and she leaned on the handlebars of her bicycle, taking deep breaths.

Using two wheels to circumnavigate her parish proved beneficial, it appeared. A month ago, there would have been a second chin.

"Two stones so far, Gus," said Clemency. "I can see you want to know, but you're too much of a gentleman to ask."

"I'm proud of you," said Gus. "You know what this means, though? When I seemed to see more of you, I see less."

"You're a terrible flirt, Gus Freeman," said Clemency.

"I'm incorrigible, according to Suzie," said Gus, "I'll leave you to your lettuce and tomatoes. I'm packing away my things and then heading home. We'll see you later. It's a lovely evening; perhaps we can sit outside in the beer garden again?"

"I'll call into the Lamb on my way home and make the arrangements," said Clemency.

She had her breath back now and rested the bicycle on the grass. Gus closed his shed door and watched the Reverend retrieve a trowel and knife from the wicker basket on the front forks.

"That knife blade should have a cover," he said as he walked towards the gate.

Gus realised Clemency would get flustered, thinking the strong arm of the law was about to descend on her shoulder.

"I never gave it a thought," she said, "will I get in trouble?"

"I won't mention it to anyone. Ask Irene for the key to Frank's shed. I don't understand why she didn't hand it over before. It would help if you didn't have to bring tools whenever you came here. Keep them locked away. I doubt there's much of value inside that old shed, anyway. A few old tools, seed boxes and empty matchboxes. Frank always spent more time smoking here than he did gardening."

"I dread to think what I'd find," said Clemency. "If there are lots of spiders, would you get rid of them for me?"

"Don't look at me," said Gus, "appeal to Irene North's sense of fair play. She should have handed you the key to the shed when you agreed to take over Frank's allotment. Get Irene to sweep it out and remove anything she wants to take home. After that, hang on until September. Pick up two conkers from the ground over there and leave them by the shed door."

"Conkers aren't big enough to drop on a spider and kill it," said Clemency.

"I'm ashamed of you, Reverend. You don't kill them. The saponin in the conkers is unpopular with spiders, lice, fleas, and ticks. They'll move on. Bert gave me that tip three years ago, and I've only seen the odd rebel since."

Gus left a chastened Clemency to her work and walked along the lane to the bungalow. He had plenty of time to shower and get dressed. But, to save time, he'd get two alternative options if Suzie objected.

Seven o'clock arrived before he knew it, and he was still ironing another spare shirt as Suzie's key slid into the lock.

"Sorry, I thought Gus Freeman lived here," said Suzie, holding the door open. "Oh, it *is* you. Someone's had a haircut. You look like a college professor trying to look as young and trendy as his students. I loved the way your hair curled over your collar. What possessed you?"

"Vera said she didn't reckon I needed a haircut when I saw her this morning. I only wanted a trim, but when I saw the price list, I thought I'd better get my money's worth."

"I got a call from Geoff Mercer today," said Suzie, "I'm off to Gablecross next Monday."

"That was my fault," said Gus.

"Geoff didn't tell me that. What did you have to do with it?"

"Gareth Francis went into his interview with Kerry

Burnside like a bull at a gate, just as I feared. I tried to warn him. I told the ACC and Geoff that it needed a woman's touch. How was I to know that Gablecross didn't have anyone of your calibre?"

"You can't sweet-talk your way around this one, Freeman," she said. "Gareth's a plonker, always has been. I must admit the variety will be welcome. Ever since the cyber course, I attended, I seem to get tagged for every job involving spending hours glued to a screen. What's that your ironing?"

"My third-choice shirt."

"Promote it to number one," said Suzie, "the colours are in your face, but it will stop people staring at your short back and sides."

Gus groaned. He could have avoided ironing the other two shirts if he'd known.

Fifteen minutes later, they left the bungalow and walked to the Lamb.

"We're not the only ones with the same idea," said Gus.

"The last time I saw a queue to get in here was New Year's Eve," said Suzie.

"Clemency Bentham was hoping to book us a table in the beer garden," said Gus as they reached the door. "I saw her earlier, just as I finished working on my allotment."

"I look forward to seeing your progress when we go there tomorrow. Glad I took the day off now. I can have as many drinks as I want tonight."

"I can't see much from where I'm standing," said Gus, "but Bert's not sat on his usual stool. Let's go outside again and enter the beer garden from the car park."

"Make your mind up," someone moaned as they battled their way to the door. Gus spotted Clemency Bentham waving when they walked into the crowded beer garden.

"Hello, the Reverend has gone all Laura Ashley," he said. "I hardly recognised her."

"Clemency's out to impress tonight," said Suzie.

"The Reverend's not the only one. Irene North's made more of an effort than usual."

"Glad you could join us, Mr Freeman," called Bert. "May I introduce my daughter, Margaret Hadlee and Brett, my David's son?"

"Good evening, Bert," said Gus. "I know I can't persuade you to call me other than Mr Freeman, but I hope Margaret and Brett will call me Gus. Welcome, both of you."

Margaret was elegant and reserved. Gus tried to remember whether he was a year older than her or a year younger. He shook her hand, and Margaret nodded a greeting.

Brett Penman was a tall, solid-looking individual. His handshake was firm and warm. The cows he treated must have loved him.

"Good to make your acquaintance, Gus. Grandpa has told us about you."

The Canadian accent was strong but educated. Gus immediately thought he could get to like the young relative of his best friend.

"Say hello to Suzie," said Bert Penman. "Mr Freeman doesn't know what to call her yet. In my day, if you hadn't gone as far as buying a ring, you referred to your young lady as your intended. Would that be the right term, Miss Ferris?"

"Close enough," she laughed. "You're a wicked man, Bert Penman."

"What have you two been doing with yourselves today?" Gus asked Margaret and Brett.

"We drove out to Stonehenge this afternoon," said Margaret.

"I hope to drive via Lacock Abbey to Bath tomorrow," said Brett. "Aunt Margaret wants to visit the Royal Crescent and the Roman Baths. Also, I'm a photography fan, so a trip to where it began and the Fox Talbot Museum is a must."

"We could go there one day, Bertie," said Irene North.

Gus noticed that Margaret frowned at that remark. Was it the pet name Irene had adopted for someone she'd known since he was a boy or because Brett had to sit beside her rather than his grandfather? Ah well, Margaret was flying home to New Zealand in a little over two days. So what was the problem if Bert and Irene found solace in spending time together in their twilight years?

There was activity all around, with customers coming and going. The pub staff looked harassed as they tried to serve drinks and food in the correct sequence. It was almost half-past eight before Bert's party ate, but the drinks arrived regularly enough to keep everyone chatting and happy.

"Never try to keep pace with Bert," Gus whispered to Brett. "He can drink anyone under the table."

"Thanks for the advice, Gus. Aunt Margaret will keep an eye on my glass. She won't want to get delayed in the morning while I recover. What *is* that lady drinking over there?"

"The Reverend? That will be an elderflower cordial. It's non-alcoholic, but she seems to enjoy it."

"Non-alcoholic? I thought the rosy cheeks were because of a full-bodied liquor I wasn't familiar with."

Gus wondered if it was the Canadian veterinary physician who was getting Clemency Bentham flustered. Perhaps that explained the Laura Ashley look.

"After I've taken Aunt Margaret to Heathrow on Saturday, I'm returning to stay with Grandpa for a few days. Aunt Margaret knows he'll be down after she leaves. He's coming to terms with our family's tragedy, but when she flies back this time, it may be the last he'll see of her. He'll never fly out to New Zealand, and she can't afford to make the trip that often. When his time is close, she wants me to call her to give her a chance to make it back in time to say goodbye."

"How long will it take for you to settle things back in Canada?" asked Gus

"Two weeks, tops," said Brett. "I set the ball rolling before we left. When I get back, Grandpa has kindly agreed to let me stay until I find a place to live."

"So you've decided to live in the UK?" said Gus.

"In the West of England," said Brett, "I plan to find a job close to the Penman home."

The food was up to its usual high standard, and everyone had a good time. Even Margaret loosened up after two sherries. Clemency Bentham helped Irene North home. Brett stayed sober to drive Margaret back to their five-star hotel in Colerne.

Bert and Margaret hugged one another before she left. Gus and Suzie stood beside Bert as the hire car disappeared.

"Do you need us to walk home with you, Bert?" asked Suzie.

"I think you two will need to help one another," laughed Bert. "I'll manage on my own as I always have. Good night to you."

Suzie stayed the night at Gus's bungalow. There was no way either of them could go anywhere.

"Did you have a good time last night?" asked Gus the following day.

"Yes, thanks. You got on famously with Brett, I noticed. Clemency didn't get a chance to see whether or not he was a churchgoer."

"Brett noticed Clemency," said Gus. "He was interested to learn why an elderflower cordial produced those rosy cheeks."

"Watch this space," said Suzie.

"Maybe. Did you notice that Margaret was standoffish? At first, I thought it was because Irene North treats Bertie as if they were an item, and she disapproved. However, Brett reminded me later that Margaret was all too aware that when she gets home to New Zealand, she's a long way from her father if he's ill."

"It's easy to believe Bert will go on forever," said Suzie. "I can see how Margaret recognised the importance of the evening. Bert just soldiers on. I don't think he's one to give things like that a thought."

"If we're going to that allotment of mine, we'd better get showered and dressed," said Gus, rolling out of bed.

"That sun's too bright," groaned Suzie.

"That's common at noon," said Gus.

Suzie heard the shower running and turned over. Gus could manage alone today.

His intended needed five minutes extra in bed.

Sunday, 1 July 2018 - Claverdon near Warwick

BLESSING UMEH WAS LEAVING her family home in Claverdon for the last time. The name came from Clover

Hill, which summed up the beautiful countryside surrounding the leafy village just five miles west of Warwick, the county town of Warwickshire.

At twenty-one, it was the first time Blessing had left home. Despite her father being a university lecturer, Blessing had no interest in school after completing her four A-levels. Instead, from the age of eleven, her ambition had always been to join the police. So since 2015, she'd made the twenty-minute drive from Claverdon to Royal Leamington Spa in her trusty Nissan Micra.

Her father, Kelechi, taught her to drive and bought her a 1997 Micra because it was a reliable runabout. After that, there was no question of Blessing owning a powerful, modern car. Kelechi thought thirty miles per hour on the road between home and work was fast enough for anyone. Some days, with the traffic on the A4189, Blessing was lucky to reach even that modest speed.

Her mother, Maryam, waved her only daughter goodbye from the front door. There were no tears because Kelechi and Maryam were also leaving home. The 'Sold' sign that stood in the garden for two months was now lying against the boundary wall waiting for collection by the estate agents. On Tuesday morning, the removals firm would arrive to transport the Umeh's belongings to their new home in Englishcombe village, four miles from Bath.

Kelechi and Maryam enjoyed village life in the English countryside, and Blessing's father had never lived far from his place of work. Claverdon was the perfect spot to commute to Warwick University, and when he secured his new lecturer's post in Bath, he wasn't searching for a house farther away than a five-mile drive.

Kelechi and Blessing had one thing in common. They both lacked a sense of direction.

Blessing passed her test first time not long after her seventeenth birthday. Her father bought the Micra for her eighteenth, weeks before she started work in Leamington. He made her drive between Claverdon and the police station every day for a week for Blessing to get used to the journey. Three years later, she knew every bump in the road, every bend and busy junction.

As a constable, she had few opportunities to drive anywhere with her duties. Because when she started working with DI Andy Carlton's team, two or three Detective Sergeants naturally believed they should jump behind the wheel due to their seniority. Blessing never complained. They would only have gotten lost if the crime had occurred somewhere she'd never visited.

Maryam was a better navigator, so Kelechi relied on his wife to know where they were going whenever they ventured out as a family. At work, he prayed that the short trip never altered enough to confuse him. Maryam often wondered how a man with such a brilliant mind in his field of expertise could be so dumb at following road signs.

That was why there were no tears that morning. Maryam had taken the precaution of purchasing a satnav for Blessing's car.

"I've entered the details," she told Blessing, "you should be at the Ferris's farm in three hours."

"I'm not using the motorway, am I?" asked Blessing. "I never feel safe."

"No, darling, I programmed it to avoid motorways. You'll be on the A429 for most of your journey. Keep calm, and you'll be fine. You can drive into Leamington Spa the same as you did before, and then the A429 takes you to Chippenham. It's almost a straight road because it follows the old Roman Fosse Way for much of the journey. Listen to the lady's voice; you can't go wrong."

"I'm nervous and excited," said Blessing.

"Of course, you are, darling. It's a new experience for you. Remember, we'll only be a few miles away from you after Tuesday. I'll get your father to drive us to Worton to meet Mr and Mrs Ferris. He wants to check if it's a suitable place for you to live. I shall accompany him because he'd never find you on his own, poor thing."

Blessing checked her mobile phone was fully charged, took one last look around the home she'd lived in for twenty-one years, got into her faithful Micra, and set off for pastures new.

Two hours later, the Fosse Way didn't seem such a good idea. The straightness of the Roman roads was legendary. People never mentioned the number of hills and vales that stood between Warwickshire and Wiltshire. Blessing felt like she'd been on a switchback ride at the fair. Up and down, her little car went, and the further she drove, the longer the inclines took. Blessing concentrated on the road ahead and every word the satnav lady said. She didn't think the sound she could hear from her trusty Micra was entirely right.

As she bypassed Malmesbury, Blessing negotiated a roundabout and slowed to take the indicated exit. She spotted a familiar sight on her left-hand side. It was a police station. Perhaps she should stop to allow her car to take a breather. When the Nissan Micra shuddered to a halt, there was something final in its tone. Blessing turned off the engine and got out.

"That doesn't look too healthy, Miss."

Blessing looked over her shoulder. A uniformed policeman had just parked behind her. He was tall, blond, and with cornflower blue eyes. Gosh, were all Wiltshire police officers as gorgeous as this? Blessing stared up at him.

"I think it's just tired after a long journey," she said.

The officer looked over her shoulder.

"I think it's more serious than that, Miss," he said.

Blessing had heard a hissing noise but dismissed it as having nothing to do with her. When she turned around, she saw steam rising from the bonnet of her little car.

"Oh no," cried Blessing, "what am I going to do?"

"There's a local garage that I can call. The owner is my brother-in-law. He doesn't charge the earth for recovery. I can put in a kind word for you if you wish."

"I've got to get to Worton," said Blessing. "If I haven't got my car, how will I get to work at London Road every day?"

"London Road, Devizes?" asked the officer, "are you a police officer?"

"Detective Constable Blessing Umeh, formerly of Warwickshire Police based in Royal Leamington Spa. Tomorrow morning, I'm to join the Crime Review Team under Mr Freeman."

"Pleased to meet you, Blessing. What a beautiful name. I'm plain old PC Dave Smith, I'm afraid. If you're working for Gus Freeman, you must be a hotshot. They only take the best from what I've heard."

"Thank you, Dave Smith. You're too kind," said Blessing. And far from being plain, she thought.

PC Smith made a call. His brother-in-law arrived with a tow truck, and Blessing removed her belongings and watched her little Micra disappear towards Malmesbury. But, based on the chin-rubbing and deep sighs, it would be a lengthy and expensive business before she got her four wheels back again.

"Right, why don't I get you tea or a coffee, and then you can call a taxi? It's probably the quickest way to get you to the other side of Devizes from here, especially on a Sunday."

"Thanks, Dave," said Blessing, "it would be a struggle to carry my case and other bags. My parents are moving to Bath on Tuesday, and they'll have the rest of my stuff in the removal van. So I'll get things I can't do without next weekend."

"I'm not working next weekend," said Dave, looking over the top of his mug of coffee.

"It's out of your way, surely?" said Blessing, trying not to stare into those blue eyes.

"Not that much. I live in Chippenham. Look, here's a list of local taxi firms. The top one is the best. Roger's a decent bloke."

"Another relative?" asked Blessing.

"Not this time," grinned Dave.

Blessing wondered if he realised how cute those dimples were.

"I can give you my mobile number," she said, "but I don't know the exact address of the farm where I'm staying. It belongs to John and Jackie Ferris of Worton."

"I know you're the detective, but I think I can find it," Dave grinned.

"Sorry, of course you will. I've just remembered. My parents are driving across at the weekend. They could bring me everything I need. I don't have to drive to Bath, thank goodness."

"That's a shame," said Dave. "Can I have that number anyway, just in case you need help with something?"

"Do you know your way around, Dave?" asked Blessing.

"You Midland girls are forward, aren't you? I've had no complaints."

Blessing realised her mistake.

"No, oh, I'm sorry. That wasn't what I meant. I easily get lost when I'm somewhere unfamiliar. I'm not sure I could find Englishcombe village from Worton. Not in an afternoon, at least."

"I can show you around the county, Blessing, and across the border into Somerset. The offer's there. Here's your ride. I'll help you with your bags and give you a ring in the week to see how you're settling in."

"I've got to sort out how to get into work in the morning yet," sighed Blessing. "Thanks for your help, Dave."

Forty-five minutes later, the taxi was driving into Devizes.

"Whereabouts is London Road?" asked Blessing.

"You turn left by the brewery," said the driver, "but we're driving straight on."

"Can you take me to the Wiltshire Police HQ, please? I'll pay the extra fare. I need to speak to someone there about tomorrow."

"Please yourself," said the driver, "it's no skin off my nose."

The car park looked ominously empty. Blessing trotted up the steps to the front door and went to Reception. She explained her predicament to the desk sergeant.

"You're staying with DI Suzie Ferris's parents then, Miss. Is that what you're telling me?"

"Yes, I have the paperwork here," said Blessing, hoping she could locate it in the depths of her handbag.

"There's nobody from the Crime Review Team here in this building, Miss. They work out of the Old Police Station seven miles from here."

72

"I remember that now," said Blessing. "I had the directions to get there from the farm ready to enter into my satnav. But now my car is in Dave's brother-in-law's garage in Malmesbury. I could hire a car, but I'd surely get lost."

"This *is* Wiltshire, Miss, and although we might appear a little backward compared to other counties, we have proper roads with signs, you know."

"You do not understand how bad my sense of direction is," sighed Blessing.

"A Detective Constable, you said, Miss, and you're working with Gus Freeman?"

The desk sergeant wondered whether there had been an error of judgement.

"I met Lydia Logan Barre when we worked on a case together," said Blessing, "I helped find Suzie Ferris's car."

"Why didn't you say. Pay off your taxi, Miss. I'll give John Ferris a call. He'll drive across in the Land Rover and collect you. If you offer to help on the farm when you've free time, he'll probably run you into work tomorrow morning. Gus Freeman can fix you up with transport after that."

Blessing ran outside to grab her gear and settle the bill with the snoozing taxi driver.

When she returned to Reception, the desk sergeant gave her the thumbs-up.

"John will be here in ten minutes, Miss. Take a seat. I hope you enjoy working with Mr Freeman. He's a character and no mistake."

Blessing thought everyone she'd met so far in Wiltshire was a character. Whatever lay ahead didn't seem as if it would be boring.

Chapter Five

Monday, 2 July 2018

GUS FREEMAN WAS LYING AWAKE, waiting for the alarm. Today was a big day in the life of the Crime Review Team. They would welcome one fresh face and the return of a prodigal son. The team had no idea what a devil of a cold case the ACC had handed them on this occasion.

Suzie Ferris had driven home to Worton yesterday evening after a meal at the Fox and Hounds. As soon as she arrived, she called Gus to tell him the latest about Blessing Umeh.

So, Blessing turned up on the doorstep at London Road like a waif and stray with her car twenty miles away? Gus wondered whether Geoff Mercer would let him borrow a spare pool car. Best not to push it. Geoff had spent a fair bit on the extra furniture in the office already. The best choice was for Neil and Luke to split the taxi duties between them until Blessing's car got repaired. He'd break the news to them later.

Gus sympathised. He knew what it meant to drive something that threatened to expire every time it travelled at over fifty miles per hour. He prayed that his beloved Focus held together for a while longer.

Gus made a mental note to call John Ferris to thank him for rescuing Blessing yesterday afternoon and delivering her to the Old Police Station this morning. There was nothing for it. He might as well smack the alarm ahead of time and get out of bed.

Thirty minutes later, he had showered, dressed and eaten. The warm July weather persuaded Gus to forego the usual fried breakfast. Suzie had unearthed a long-lost waffle maker at the back of a cupboard on Saturday. Tess must have bought it years ago and decided Gus wasn't ready for such excitement because he couldn't recall it ever getting used.

The discovery prompted Suzie to berate Gus about waffles being second on the list of the ten worst things you could choose for breakfast. Then she checked that they had enough eggs and other ingredients to create at least three alternative recipes.

After testing Suzie's three versions, Gus agreed the waffle maker could stay on the worktop for the odd occasion he craved variety in his diet.

"If you're going to die early," Suzie said, "at least you won't die of boredom."

It had been that sort of weekend.

They'd wasted the best part of Thursday recovering from the night before with Bert, and then on Friday, Suzie was working. Gus joined Bert on the allotment mid-morning, and after a full day's work, his old friend agreed Gus was now less than a week behind schedule.

As Gus leaned on his fork, feeling every one of his sixty-two years, he thought he could live with getting that close. When Suzie arrived at seven o'clock, she found him asleep in the chair. With the weekend ahead to do as they pleased, she poured a red wine, sat next to him, and waited until he stirred.

"Pizza?" she asked when he opened an eye.

"Chinese," he replied. Suzie made the call. Gus shook himself awake, refilled her glass and poured one for himself. They were in bed by ten.

Gus had read through the Ursula Wakeley murder file while Suzie returned home for her morning ride on Saturday morning. He pencilled in a visit to Mere for early next week. He'd driven past it frequently but never visited Shaftesbury Road. Gus wanted to get a sense of the murder site.

He and Suzie spent the afternoon at the bungalow. Gus tidied the garden, and Suzie re-organised his kitchen cupboards. Both of them made surprising discoveries. Suzie found the waffle maker. Gus found Tess's roses thriving on the bungalow wall and decided they needed more trellis to spread their wings further.

A meal at the Waggon & Horses rounded off a good Saturday. When they surfaced on Sunday, the conversation returned to what faced them over the next few weeks.

"I don't suppose I'll have a separate room at Gable-cross," said Suzie.

"The detective squad office is deep in the building's heart," said Gus. "I imagine you'll get partnered with Gareth Francis. Don't worry. I trust you."

"If you can't trust your intended, then there's no future for a relationship."

"Very true," said Gus. "Of course, re-organising a

chap's cupboards could be considered presumptuous unless it was confirmation of commitment."

"I must give that thought while playing kneesies with Gareth."

That was yesterday. At half-past eight on a sunny Monday morning, Gus closed the front door behind him, gave an admiring glance around his garden and fired up the Focus. There wasn't the same throaty roar that Gene Hunt achieved with his Quattro, but Gus reckoned today was that kind of day.

When he arrived at the rear of the Old Police Station building to find all four of the team's reserved parking spaces filled, the Eighties euphoria faded fast. Gus knew he'd forgotten to mention it to Geoff Mercer. The Crime Review Team needed two extra permanent parking spaces. Naturally, locals would protest, but who offered them the land in the first place?

The spot in the middle of town was a prime piece of real estate. Wiltshire Police had occupied the building for over a century before leasing the ground floor to two charity shops. The High Street that the Council was keen to protect needed shoppers driving into town. Could two spaces jeopardise the town's future? Gus reversed the Focus into one of the remaining empty spots and got out.

He spotted a familiar Land Rover on the other side of the car park. John Ferris wasn't searching for a place to park; he was dropping off his lodger. Gus waved a hand, but John was in a hurry to return to the farm. Blessing Umeh took hesitant steps towards the lift doors.

"Welcome to the Old Police Station, Blessing," said Gus. "That's it, call the lift, and we can travel together to meet your new colleagues. We're both cutting it fine today. Everyone else arrived well before nine."

"I didn't want to be late on my first day, Mr Freeman," said Blessing. "Mrs Ferris insisted I eat a hearty breakfast, and her husband was back from the barn five minutes later than he'd promised her. I'm so sorry."

Gus laughed.

"That's not unusual, Blessing; you'll soon adjust to country life. Unfortunately, it operates on a different time clock from everyone else. Suzie explained your exploits yesterday. Don't worry; I'll get one of the lads to collect you and drop you back at the farm until your car's fixed."

"The way my little Micra sounded yesterday, I'm afraid it might be terminal," said Blessing as they travelled up to the first floor.

"We'll cross that bridge when we come to it," said Gus, "forget it for now. Let's get you introduced to the rest of the team."

After the introductions, Blessing Umeh took her seat at the spare desk and took in the Crime Review Team office's features. It was better equipped than the detective squad room she'd left behind in Royal Leamington Spa. Maybe that was due to the time the two offices had been operating.

This office hadn't gained many bumps and scrapes to its furniture and fittings in the few months they'd been here. The Newbold Terrace station had been running for eight years. Blessing realised she needed to be careful not to spill coffee over her keyboard once a week as she had back there.

"This wasn't how I saw my retirement years," said Gus, "but here we are at the start of a new week with a new member of staff and a new case. Alex is back with us again, and the first thing I have to tell him is to jump in your car, mate, and head for London Road. The Acting Chief Constable wants you to join the Hub. There's just one item on your list. Match the red-headed sniper on the rooftop of the Cheney Manor Industrial Estate building back in 2013 to a person in the database. I was hoping you could give me a name for Grant Burnside's killer. If he doesn't fit with anyone ever arrested, then be creative. Perhaps you need to look for a military connection. Skill with a rifle from a distance takes practice. Check local gun clubs and farmers with a valid firearms licence who might have held a grudge. Anything that opens up a list of possible names."

"Do we know for certain the guy was English?" asked Luke.

"Fair comment," said Gus. "You must liaise with Geoff Mercer, Alex. Get him to contact the right people to access former military personnel in the UK before 2013. They might have been a hired gun, or it could go deeper. For example, Grant Burnside operated in mainland Europe way back before the gang majored in drugs in their home town. The hitman could have picked up the contract abroad."

"What about that Curran bloke you crossed swords with, guv," said Neil. "Would it be worth calling him?"

"Download the necessary data from the Freeman Files, Alex. You'll find everything you need there. Once you've exhausted every option I outlined, then, and only then, will we go cap in hand to Brendan bleeding Curran and the Organised Crime Task Force. Give me a shout when you're ready to leave. I'll come with you. I can park my car in its rightful spot."

"We're short in that department," said Luke.

"I'll sort it with DS Mercer," said Gus. "Alex will be absent for a while. Now's as good a time as any to ask you and Neil to arrange a schedule with Blessing. Her car died on the trip south yesterday. It's stuck in a garage in Malmesbury until they decide whether it's worth operating. You both know your way to the Ferris's farm in Worton."

"Yes, guv," replied Neil and Luke.

"I'll take Blessing home tonight," said Luke.

"I'll collect her in the morning, guv," said Neil. "Any chance you can creep out early tomorrow morning and pinch a few fresh eggs, Blessing?"

"Have they got chickens?" asked Blessing, "I haven't heard them squawking."

"Neil's pulling your leg," said Gus, "it's one of his bad habits. Are you ready, Alex? Let's get this parking reshuffle sorted, and I can run through the new case with the others."

When they were in the lift, Gus apologised for the brief notice.

"The Hub business cropped up last week when I'd sent the others home for a few days' rest."

"That's okay, guv. I'm working on a cold case, and that's why I joined this team. Lydia described what kept crawling out from under stones as you tried to get a lead on who killed this Burnside character. You couldn't ignore them, and you got several excellent results for your endeavours. It just so happened that the one you started with wasn't among them. It doesn't matter when we solve them as long as we do."

"I've trained you well, Alex," said Gus. "It's great to see you fit and well. You left the stick at home today. Is that goodbye to it now?"

"I get the odd twinge now and again, guv," said Alex.

"Tell me about it," said Gus.

He started walking towards his Focus and then stopped.

"Alex, I don't think Lydia did more than give Blessing a brief welcome this morning. She's not usually so quiet. Is everything okay?"

"We spent time in London searching for her father during our time off, guv. Eleanor, her mother, gave Lydia her father's name the last time she went to Glasgow. It was slow progress, but we found his ship. It sailed on to Rotterdam from Edinburgh. Chidozie Barre, that's his name, worked for the same Greek shipping company until 2007. Then the trail went cold. His ship sank in the South China Sea, and after being rescued and put ashore in Da Nang, Vietnam, it seems as if he decided enough was enough. Unless he joined another company, he didn't go to sea again. So next weekend we will start again. Lydia's determined to find her Dad. The trouble is, after what we found last week. I think Lydia's worried about what we'll learn."

"Thanks for the tip, Alex. I'll tread warily," said Gus. "Good luck with the whiz kids at the Hub. Keep an eye out for Kassie Trotter. You can't miss her. She'll let you sample her sticky buns if you feel peckish by three o'clock this afternoon."

When Gus returned to the office, Luke and Lydia were alone.

"Where did Neil and Blessing disappear?"

"Neil offered to explain the Gaggia to her, guv," said Luke. "We're getting treated to an early coffee."

"Did Neil mention anything before I arrived earlier?" asked Gus, crossing his fingers behind his back.

"Melody's back home," said Lydia.

"And Neil's not in the dog house, guv," said Luke.

"Everyone seems to have had excitement since I saw you last," said Gus.

"You should have gone to Specsavers, guv," said Lydia.

"Are you having a pop at my haircut? I got enough earache from Suzie."

"No, guv. It's growing back already. Don't worry. Luke had his own excitement too."

Luke raised his left hand.

"Nicky and I haven't set a date yet, but we've taken the first step."

"Congratulations, both of you," said Gus.

Gus noticed Blessing and Neil were back in the room with the coffees.

"Sorry, Blessing, you'll get to know the ins and outs of our everyday tale of country coppers in time. I think I should walk through our next case with you all. The others know what's required. After the crime scene photos are up on the boards and the list of characters and their backgrounds added to the whiteboards, perhaps Lydia will show you how to access the Freeman Files on your computer."

"Which part of the county are we looking at, guv?" asked Lydia.

"Mere, a small town that lies at the extreme southwestern tip of Salisbury Plain," said Gus. "It's close to the borders with Somerset and Dorset. It was on my patch when I worked in Salisbury, but I never had cause to go there. I passed it many times. Before I became a detective, they built a bypass on the northern edge of the town. Before that, the A303 trunk road went straight through the town."

"Is it as big a town as this one?" asked Blessing, "I've never heard of it."

"Three thousand inhabitants, give or take," said Gus, "so a small town with an older population than the average. The Methodist Church started as a Primitive Methodist chapel in the middle of the nineteenth century. There was a school in that building for many years. The church was deconsecrated last year and is now getting converted for residential use. It might be strange to mention the church, but it might play a part in the case that we're investigating."

"Are there many churches in Mere, guv?" asked Neil.

"No more than usual. St Michael's is the oldest, and parts of that building date back to the thirteenth century. St Michael's has one unusual claim to fame: ten misericords."

"What's one of those when it's at home?" asked Neil.

"A mercy seat," said Blessing Umeh, "it's designed so you can fold down the seat and rest when you've knelt in prayer for hours on end."

"Well, you learn something new every day," said Neil.

"The town's library and the museum moved into an old National School building in 1970. Our victim worked there when she left school and again after her parents died."

"Who was our victim, guv," asked Lydia.

Gus handed out copies of the murder file to each team member.

"Inside the front cover, you'll see that I've included a summary of the original investigation led by DCI Melvin Jefferson and DI Fabian Kite from Salisbury. I knew both officers when I worked there. I wanted to work on this case, but Jefferson assigned me to another job two weeks before the murder."

"A pity," said Neil, "we probably wouldn't be looking at this file now."

"Jefferson was a good detective, Neil. If he missed something, then it was well hidden."

Gus waited for a minute while the summary got absorbed.

"Ursula Wakeley died five years ago on the night of the sixteenth of January. Ms Wakeley was seventy-eight, a spinster who lived alone in a bungalow on Shaftesbury Road. We have a street map of the area in the murder file. Blessing, get that map on one wallboard, please. It will help us understand the movements of various people the police interviewed."

"Did Ursula Wakeley own a car, guv?" asked Luke.

"No, and there's no garage at the bungalow. Ursula's parents never drove. Her brother, Arthur, eighty-five now, handed in his licence in 2015 after colliding with a bollard in Morrison's car park. He decided it was too risky to keep driving. I don't know when he passed his test, but I assume he parked on the road or the wide pathway leading to the bungalow. Again, photographs of the property are in the file. The nearest neighbours were around one hundred yards from the Wakeley family home. There were open fields opposite in 2013. Nobody heard a thing."

"How did Ms Wakeley get into town, guv?" asked Neil, "that road doesn't look as if it was on a bus route."

"The town centre is a twenty-minute walk from the bungalow," said Gus, "which for someone of Ursula's generation isn't as daunting as it would be for you, Neil. I looked at the file at the weekend and plan to visit the murder site tomorrow. A garden shed to the side of the bungalow was mentioned. Perhaps when they were younger, Arthur and Ursula owned bicycles. Who knows?"

"Had the victim always lived at this address?" asked Lydia.

"She had," said Gus, "it wasn't uncommon in those days for the youngest daughter to assume a carer's duties for elderly parents. In this case, her father Gideon dropped dead in 1966, leaving his widow, Elspeth, looking at twenty or thirty years on her own. Arthur already had a young family and was an assistant bank manager. Ursula worked at the library in town, but she was single. Ursula quit her job and stayed with her mother. Elspeth died in 1996."

"These crime scene photos are horrific," said Luke, "I won't forget these in a hurry."

"Nevertheless, I want them posted on a whiteboard,

Luke. The killer stabbed our victim in the heart between ten o'clock and midnight. What happened on either side of that is a mystery. Not just what happened, but why?"

"The original investigation deemed this was a burglary," asked Blessing. "Was that a mistake? The violence seems excessive."

"I can understand why Jefferson followed the trail of the missing jewellery. Consider the victim for a moment— an elderly lady living alone without near neighbours. The burglar could watch the place without raising suspicion and check the level of security. When you dig deeper, you'll learn that the victim never closed her curtains in any room in the house. So, the burglar knew Ursula was home alone. They broke in through the kitchen and carried out the initial attack. Forensic evidence showed that the burglar took a large knife from the kitchen and whacked Ursula over the head with a weighty object they grabbed from a sideboard in the living room. Then they dragged Ursula into her bedroom, stripped her naked, and began rifling the drawers of her dressing table looking for valuables."

"The file says there was no sexual motive to the crime," said Blessing, "why did they humiliate her by stripping her naked?"

"Before I put forward my suggestions," said Gus, "does anyone have something to offer?"

"They kept Ms Wakeley alive to find out where the valuables were, guv," said Neil. "Murder wasn't what they planned to carry out. They used the kitchen knife to threaten her, nothing more."

"Two thousand pounds worth of jewellery isn't a great haul," said Luke. "Maybe the burglar believed there was something of greater value in the house. You know, rumours in the town that her father didn't trust banks and had a fortune in cash under the floorboards."

"It was someone local then, guv," said Neil, "that's what your former colleagues thought. When that young woman tried flogging jewellery in Ringwood, they put two and two together."

"And made five," said Gus. "If the jewellery they found disappointed the robbers, why didn't they search the house after they stabbed her? Ursula's handbag was in plain sight in the living room. When Jefferson followed the burglary angle, I believe the most important aspect got overlooked."

"Why not stab her and have done with it?" asked Neil.

"There had to be more to it than that," said Blessing.

"You've studied this file in more detail than we have just yet, guv," said Lydia. "Can I walk through the sequence of events, and you correct me when I go astray?"

"Go ahead," said Gus.

"The break-in occurred at around ten. Ursula didn't hear the commotion in the kitchen when the burglar smashed the glass panel in the back door. Whoever it was, they opened drawers in the kitchen to find a suitable knife and entered the living room. Ursula still didn't react. The intruder picked up a horse statue and hit her on the back of the head, knocking her out. Why didn't she turn around? Was she stone deaf?"

"There was nothing to suggest she suffered from impaired hearing," said Gus. "Her handyman, Don Hillier, Monica Butterworth, from the library, and her brother and sister-in-law gave statements to that effect."

"You said the curtains were never closed," said Neil, "so was someone at the front of the house distracting her?"

"That fits with the notion that two teenagers committed the burglary," said Lydia.

"It leaves us with a problem, though," said Gus.

"The unnecessary violence," said Blessing.

"Continue with your sequence of events, Lydia," said Gus.

"When Ursula was unconscious, the one that broke in opened the door for their accomplice. That made it easier to move her through to the bedroom. The young man did the lifting, and the woman carried the knife. One pulled out drawers on the dressing table while the other stripped Ursula. The fatal blow took place somewhen in the next two hours. Do you think they tortured her, guv?"

"There's no evidence of that. The only injury that occurred before the stabbing was the whack to the head. The knife wound to the heart was a fatal blow. Ursula died in minutes."

"Why didn't they just search the house and leave?" asked Luke.

"What came next, Lydia?" asked Gus.

"The young woman, well, I assume it was the woman, cleaned the horse statue and put it back on the sideboard with the other statue and the clock. Meanwhile, the young man continued to use the knife on the dead body, as seen in the crime scene photos."

"What else can you see on the photos in the murder file?" asked Gus.

"The Scenes of Crimes Officer took a photo of the living room window, guv," said Neil, "with the curtains drawn halfway across the window."

"What does that tell us?"

"The young woman drew the curtains before they left," said Lydia.

"Did SOCO take photos of the front bedroom window?"

"I can't see one, guv."

"Odd that, don't you think? The killer left the body cut to ribbons in a frenzied attack after the poor woman died, in full view of anyone walking along Shaftesbury Road the next morning. Yet they attempted to draw the ones in the living room."

"Ursula Wakeley drew the curtains," said Neil.

"That explains the query Lydia had," said Luke, "about why Ursula had heard no one breaking in."

"And why the blow to the head came from behind her," said Blessing. "Someone outside who scared her to death. Sorry, you know what I meant. She must have been terrified."

"I've read this thing through several times," said Gus, "and Lydia has the important steps in the right order. I'm unsure when the clean-up got carried out or who did it. For instance, the female could have left with the jewellery before the man stabbed Ursula. When we analysed the initial events of the break-in, it was plain they had brought the thick cloth with them to avoid cutting themselves on the glass. However, they didn't bring a weapon. They used what was to hand. That suggested murder wasn't on the cards until much later. As Blessing said, the face at the window terrified Ursula, as did the blow to the head, and she found herself naked when she recovered consciousness. The young man may have told his accomplice he'd tie Ursula up, make sure there were no clues left for the police, and then get off home."

"Surely, Ursula could identify them," said Blessing. "They couldn't let her live."

"Neither person seemed to care about that, guv," said Luke. "Ursula must have seen both of them when she came around."

"Unless they wore masks," said Neil.

"That was my thought too, Neil," said Gus, "a ski mask, or one of those grotesque character masks would frighten an elderly lady if it suddenly appeared at her window."

"Hang on," said Lydia, "if they wore masks, there was no need to kill her."

"We're getting to the crux of it, aren't we?" said Gus. "We don't know whether they both stayed throughout the ordeal, but a jewellery theft wasn't the true reason for the terror they inflicted. There was no reason to kill her if she couldn't identify them. So what can we deduce from the facts we have?"

"Ursula knew her attackers, guv," said Luke.

"The jewellery was a ploy to fool the police into thinking it was a robbery," said Neil.

"Murder was the endgame they planned all along," said Lydia.

"Three correct assumptions and a bonus point," said Gus.

"But how do we explain the mutilation that occurred post-mortem?" asked Blessing.

"We discover what Ursula did that prompted such a heinous act," said Gus.

Chapter Six

GUS LEFT the team to fill the walls and whiteboards with items from the murder file. Once that was complete, he could get Luke to compile a list of interviewees. Who should come with him tomorrow for the walk around the murder site?

Lydia was the obvious choice. She might think of something a mere man would miss, and he could chat quietly with her away from the others.

Luke Sherman posted the crime scene photos onto a whiteboard. As he worked, he couldn't avoid looking at what they contained. Luke prided himself on having a robust constitution, and the sight of blood didn't phase him. However, the images from Ursula Wakeley's bedroom were extremely gruesome. He looked beyond the gore and tried to imagine how a person could do this to another human being.

Disturbed didn't go anywhere near far enough.

Luke let his mind wander.

Gus suggested that a remote location such as this was ideal for a criminal to watch for weeks while they devised a plan that guaranteed success. What about the curtains? There had been no sexual element to the attack, according to the murder file. Ursula's bungalow on Shaftesbury Road seemed perfect for a Peeping Tom. Ursula kept her curtains open year-round. Did she dress or undress with the light on in winter?

Luke reflected on other cases he'd investigated where sick individuals progressed from voyeurism to physical assault. In extreme cases, it was the precursor to murder. On the other hand, some killers started young, killing domestic animals before attacking a man or woman. Was this what they saw at work here?

"Was there a Peeping Tom, a stalker, or pet killer in the town, guv?" he asked.

Gus looked up from his computer.

"I don't know. Check it out. I don't remember reading anything in the file. So either Jefferson and his team didn't find anyone or discounted the idea because of the robbery angle."

"It's there, guv, towards the back," said Neil. "Nobody with that record lived in Mere or anywhere in the Salisbury district. Did the coroner give any sign about the wounds Ursula suffered after death?"

"In what way, Neil?" asked Gus.

"Any degree of hesitation, for instance. You expect that for a first-timer."

"Excellent point. Let me call up that report," said Gus. "Where are we? Right, here we go, nothing conclusive. The coroner remarked that the killer seemed to experiment with the body. Cuts varied in depth and length. Several were close together on the left arm, and on the right, they played a game of noughts and crosses. The slashes grew more violent on the torso and upper thighs. Assuming the killer started at the top and worked down, there's an increasing confidence level. But, of course, that's only my interpretation of what I see. I'm no medical expert."

"Will they kill again?" asked Lydia.

"Who's saying they haven't," said Neil.

"Well, there's no record of anything remotely similar in this region in the past five years," said Gus.

"Should we widen the net, guv?" asked Luke.

"If the murder were planned, the urge to kill again would be strong," said Lydia. "Does that mean we're looking for a serial killer?"

"Far too soon to say, Lydia," said Gus, "we've only got one death. This murder was planned, yes, but I suspect it was personal. The two people involved took retribution against Ursula Wakeley for something she did to them."

"What would an old librarian have done to get someone that angry, guv?" asked Luke.

"Hard to imagine a fine for the late return of a book or a telling off for chatting in the library being the catalyst, guv," said Neil.

"Thank you, Neil," said Gus. "Jefferson and Kite interviewed the neighbours, Ursula's family, library colleagues and church friends. Nobody remembered arguments or anything unusual in the weeks leading up to the murder."

"Did those people have corroborated alibis?" asked Luke.

Gus nodded.

"We're positive it wasn't a sex crime?" asked Lydia.

"There was no semen, but that didn't mean they didn't try," said Neil.

"The body showed zero sexual activity, Neil. Ursula was virgo intacta."

"Right, understood, guv. What about people that might have visited Shaftesbury Road to carry out surveillance during daylight hours? They seem to have done it without raising suspicion. We know about her handyman, but did she have a van delivery in the recent past, a tradesperson calling by, or other foot traffic that people might notice?"

"Ursula's postman would be a regular sight, meaning that he didn't stand out," said Blessing. "I suppose he got checked, did he?"

"He did," said Gus.

"It had to be someone nobody thought unusual," said Lydia. "Who might that be? Someone who looked perfectly normal and had every right to be there."

"A boy scout on Bob-A Job-Week?" asked Neil.

"I thought that was before your time, Neil," said Luke.

"I haven't told you the downside of getting a cold case where the victim and the witnesses were ancient," sighed Gus.

"Most of our interviews will need to be held through a medium, guv,"

"Exactly, Neil."

"Do I compile a list of those still alive, guv?" asked Luke. "As we think there was a personal element, surely the family and her handyman can't offer anything useful."

"I'm wary of jumping to conclusions on this one, Luke. We'll follow our usual pattern but try to tease a forgotten memory or impression from each person we interview. They might point us in a different direction. I've had a thought for tomorrow. We'll meet at my place at nine o'clock. Lydia, you can drive. Neil, collect Blessing from Ferris's farm as arranged. Luke, you hold the fort while we're away and get interview dates and times sorted. Contact the victim's brother and Don Hillier now. I want to meet Arthur tomorrow at ten o'clock and the handyman at eleven. When we return in the early afternoon, we'll get our impressions into the Freeman Files, reassess our approach to the case and allocate interviews."

"Do you want me to contact ex-DCI Jefferson and ex-DI Kite, guv?" asked Luke.

"Concentrate on Mel Jefferson out of the two of them, Luke. Let's get his thoughts on how Fabian Kite handled himself as part of that conversation. Also, don't forget to ask what pressures he had on him. I was running a major robbery case. Resources would have been stretched across the department. Perhaps the Assistant Chief Constable applied top-down pressure for Mel to move on quicker than he preferred. I can't recall what else we had on our caseload back then. There was always something."

"Will we do much walking, guv?" asked Lydia.

"Sensible shoes tomorrow, Lydia," said Gus. "You know me, distances between different points relating to the potential suspects and the murder site are important, and seeing the places where the victim lived, worked and worshipped often starts a niggle."

Blessing looked at Lydia's four-inch heels and her flat lace-up shoes. She wished she had the confidence to dress like Lydia, but with her luck, she'd twist an ankle or fall flat on her face if she ever tried wearing heels that high.

What her strict father would say didn't bear thinking about.

The Crime Review Team worked in silence. The crime scene photos loomed over them from the whiteboard, and the lifeless eyes of Ursula Wakeley sat in judgement, urging each of them to find her killer.

Lydia Logan Barre wouldn't forget the picture of the victim seated on her bed, with her back against the headboard. Gus reckoned it was too early to say they were hunting a serial killer. Lydia thought the killer posed the body deliberately. As if they knew the forensic team would take that particular photo and its effect on everyone who saw it.

Whoever carried out this murder, Lydia hoped she never met them.

Tuesday, 3 July 2018

GLENDA WAKELEY HAD GIVEN up trying to explain to her sister-in-law, Ursula, that there was a good reason for her daughter Sam's single life. The only blessing was that the God-fearing Gideon hadn't lived long enough to learn that the infant he read Bible stories to had lived with the same woman since she reached eighteen. Her father-in-law would have imploded.

As for her mother-in-law, Elspeth worried more over her health and keeping her daughter close at hand. So, the issue never needed an explanation. After the phone call she'd received yesterday afternoon from Detective Sergeant Luke Sherman; they had to relive the nightmare of Ursula's death again. Arthur wasn't in the best of health. Who was at eighty-five?

Glenda hoped it would be a brief meeting. Nothing had changed in five years. She was still miserable but resigned to her fate. The only consolation of seeing out her days with Arthur was that they didn't lack money. If they ran short, they always had the bungalow. Arthur refused to go inside again after the day he discovered Ursula's body.

Arthur used a local firm to make sure the fabric of the building remained secure. He refused to rent it out or sell it. Nobody would ever live in it while Arthur lived. It could stay boarded up forever, as far as he was concerned.

The front doorbell rang, and Glenda checked her watch. At ten o'clock, at least, they arrived on time.

"Good morning, Mrs Wakeley," said Gus Freeman. "My colleague and I were admiring your garden."

"You'd better come in," said Glenda, ignoring the comment, "Arthur's in the lounge. It would help if you spoke up. Arthur's hearing's not good."

Gus and Lydia followed Glenda into the living room. The three-bedroomed detached home sat in a quiet cul-de-sac of sixteen houses. Gus checked the latest valuations yesterday. You wouldn't get much change out of six hundred thousand pounds. The retired banker had taken advantage of the reduced mortgage interest rates that the High Street banks offered their employees.

Arthur Wakeley remained seated. He looked up from his morning paper but didn't understand why someone was calling on him.

"Who's this, Glenda?" he asked.

"The police, Arthur. I reminded you at breakfast that they were coming. They want to talk about Ursula."

"My sister's dead," said Arthur.

"My name is Freeman, Mr Wakeley," said Gus, "and my colleague is Ms Barre. Wiltshire Police didn't find your sister's killer five years ago, but no case is ever closed. It's time to try again."

"I don't want to go back," said Arthur.

"We'll only ask a few questions," said Lydia. "Why don't

your wife and I pop into the kitchen and make us a cup of tea or coffee? You can chat with Mr Freeman."

Lydia steered Glenda Wakeley towards the doorway into the hall. Gus heard the kettle getting filled and cupboard doors opening. Good girl. Now he could have a go at getting sense out of Ursula's brother.

"I've never talked about what I saw in front of Glenda," said Arthur. "It was horrific."

"Let's talk of more pleasant memories, Arthur. What was life like for you and Ursula growing up?"

"We had to do as we were told," said Arthur, "our father was strict. Spare the rod and spoil the child. He believed that alright. I stopped going to church as soon as he died. I didn't dare miss a church service while he was alive."

"How did he discipline you? Did he treat Ursula the same way?"

"He made us cut the wood from the hazel trees in the field behind the bungalow. That was part of the punishment. We made the blessed switches ourselves."

"You both went to school in the town, I believe?"

"We had no choice but to follow in our parent's footsteps and go to the Methodist school. Things got better after we went to the school in Gillingham when we reached eleven."

"A bus journey every day?" said Gus.

"It meant we stayed away from home for longer," said Arthur. "Less time to make him mad enough to lash out again. In the long summer school holidays, he worked in the fields for twelve hours, so it wasn't as bad."

"You both left school at the same time. Why was that?"

"I was eighteen and had passed my A-levels. I'd travelled up to London on the train at the start of the summer term for an interview to join Lloyd's Bank. The interview was successful, and I started work in the Mere branch. Ursula had sat her O-levels, and her father decided she'd had enough schooling. What point was there, filling her mind with unhealthy ideas when she would soon get married and have children? He said you didn't need schooling for that."

"Ursula worked at the library, didn't she?" said Gus.

Glenda and Lydia returned from the kitchen with two teas and two coffees. There were no biscuits.

"She ruled the roost there for years," said Glenda. "They were glad to see the back of her."

"That's not fair, Glenda," said Arthur, "she did her best to get people to behave correctly for a library. It's not a meeting room. They used to hang 'Silence' signs every-where in the old days. Now it's a free-for-all."

"How do you know, you silly old fool? When was the last time you stepped inside the library?"

Gus and Lydia sat sipping their coffees and let the storm abate. It's incredible what you could learn over a cup of coffee.

"If schooling was unhealthy, Arthur," said Gus, "I'm surprised Gideon allowed his daughter to work in a library. She would have access to far more liberal ideas than at secondary school."

"My father read nothing other than the Bible," said Arthur. "He didn't believe a person needed more to lead a good life."

"Whenever we visited them with our children, Matthew and Samantha, Gideon read them Bible stories," said Glenda. "You won't find another book or magazine in that bungalow."

"Glenda was telling me in the kitchen that they still own

the bungalow, guv," said Lydia quietly. "We can have the key to look around it if we wish."

"That will be a big help," said Gus. "Arthur, was there nobody that came calling on Ursula? Were there no boys she met at school that showed an interest? What about the youth club or someone from another family in your congregation?"

"Father's reputation discouraged anyone I knew in town from coming around," said Arthur. "We got told to come straight home after school. There was no loitering in the road chatting with other children. I met Glenda at school, and there was never anyone else for either of us. Father was content with my choice. He was over-protective with Ursula, though. She went to church gatherings, but one or both of our parents was always monitoring her. She told me once that boys came to watch her when she worked at the library. Ursula was an attractive girl in many ways. Whether anyone plucked up the courage to ask her out, I don't know. She never said. I was married, and my job took us away from the town for a while. Not long after we returned, father dropped dead, and mother told me she couldn't cope without him. So, I asked Ursula to stay home until my mother regained her strength."

"My mother-in-law had no intention of letting Ursula get married," said Glenda. "She wanted her to stay at home forever. Ursula was my best friend at school, Mr Freeman. She was old-fashioned in her ways and opinions, but her upbringing shaped her. If Ursula had stayed at school, she would have been clever enough to attend university. She was brighter than Arthur. Instead, Ursula's life got stifled by her parents' religious zeal. She could have had a career, a husband, and a family if Arthur hadn't insisted she quit her job at thirty-one to become Elspeth's carer."

"I did what I thought best," said Arthur, "it was what my father wanted."

"Rubbish," said Glenda, "you were jealous of her intellect, and we'd returned to Mere because the bank realised you were incompetent. You did it out of spite."

"Perhaps you could look out that key for the bungalow?" asked Gus. He'd heard enough to form a broader opinion on the life Ursula Wakeley led. And far too much of the life Arthur and Glenda enjoyed.

Glenda walked through the hallway. A bunch of keys hung on the end peg of a coat rack on the wall beside the front door.

"There you are, Mr Freeman," she said, "Front door, back door, and shed key."

"We'll return them when we've finished, Mrs Wakeley," said Gus.

"No rush," she replied, "We won't be going anywhere near that place. You'll find it's boarded up, and the electricity's off now. Arthur has a local firm go round there regularly to maintain the bungalow and dissuade squatters. He gave strict instructions to remove perishable items but to leave everything else alone."

Gus was halfway out of the front door when he turned back.

"What was your husband's reaction to Ursula returning to the library after a thirty-year gap?" asked Lydia.

"He couldn't believe they wanted her," said Glenda. "Perhaps those who worked with her before had retired. Ursula would have been hard-working and diligent. I can guarantee that. I expect Monica Butterworth put up with Ursula's foibles because the younger ones she has now are a lazy bunch, only interested in the computers they have."

Gus thought Neil and Blessing would have a tale to tell

when they got back to the Old Police Station. This trip could prove more productive than he'd first thought.

"How did your sister-in-law spend her evenings and weekends?" asked Gus.

"Ursula read a lot and watched television. Only certain programmes, of course. Mind you; I can only tell you what she told me. We didn't visit one another's homes. We met in town at a café; or restaurant for special occasions such as a birthday or Christmas."

"Why didn't you come with Arthur that day?" asked Lydia. "There was only a suspicion that Ursula had come to harm. She might have preferred another woman to help her if it had been a fall. Especially her best friend at school."

"Arthur wouldn't let me," said Glenda, "Charles Marshall called him, told him what Don Hillier had seen, and he left the house in a rage."

"What made him angry?" asked Gus.

"He was getting ready to go out. Arthur dreaded Ursula turning into their mother. He kept worrying that we might end up caring for her."

"When you learned the truth, was there anyone you suspected might have killed Ursula?" asked Gus.

"The police asked us that five years ago. I told them that Ursula was still my friend, even though she could be objectionable. I could never harm her, and nor could Arthur. There were plenty in town that she'd upset with comments she made at church, in the library or passing. No matter how wounding those remarks might be, they wouldn't be enough for someone to kill her. How could they?"

Lydia went to the lounge to collect the cups and saucers while Gus chatted with Glenda.

Arthur was reading the newspaper.

"Did you ever drive past your old home, Mr Wakeley? Even if you weren't dropping in to see your sister?"

"I hadn't forgotten where it was, young lady," said Arthur. "I'd have to go out of my way to drive along Shaftesbury Road. It never appealed to me."

"I wondered if you had seen anyone hanging around, looking as if they were up to no good."

"Don Hillier would have told me if he thought there was something I should know. He was there often enough, and he never mentioned it."

"To find your sister's body the way you did was a dreadful shock," said Lydia, "but did it come as a surprise that someone killed her?"

"What sort of question is that?" shouted Arthur.

"Was Ursula adept at hurting people with words," said Lydia.

"She wasn't always so vicious," he replied.

"Did Ursula pick on anyone in particular?"

"No, after mother died, I noticed she was more bitter and less forgiving than when she was younger. Those years of caring for her mother took their toll. My sister could be nasty to anyone."

Lydia left Arthur to his paper, placed the cups and saucers on the kitchen worktop, and rejoined Gus and Glenda in the hallway.

"All done, ready to go?" Gus asked.

"Yes, guv, just saying goodbye to Mr Wakeley."

Glenda watched them walk down the driveway to a red Mini and then closed the door. With luck, that would be the last they'd see of them. They could drop the keys through the letterbox for all she cared.

"What did we learn from that then, Lydia?" asked Gus as he sat beside her.

"Three things off the top of my head. You were right that religion played a role in the case, guv," said Lydia. "Glenda would have left Arthur twenty years ago if he hadn't got a good pension. Also, our quiet librarian had a knack for insulting people everywhere she went."

"We're no closer to isolating a suspect or where any suspects might originate."

"Where to next, guv?"

"Need you ask?"

"We told Don Hillier we wanted to see him at eleven, guv. I know you; once we get into that bungalow, we'll be there all day."

"In that case, let's pick him up and take him with us. We'll chat as he runs through his part in the morning's proceedings."

"Do you think he'll go for that, guv? I know the bedroom's clean, but it might be traumatic for him."

"I'll swear blind that I never said this if anyone asks," said Gus, "but it might get Hillier to say something he wouldn't do if he were in his comfy armchair."

"Sneaky, guv," said Lydia. "Why didn't I think of that?"

Lydia was right. Don Hillier *was* reticent about stepping inside the bungalow. He came out of his house and stood by the door of the Mini. Gus had squeezed in the back and was regretting not driving his Focus.

"It's not because of what happened," he said. "I'll be waiting for Ursula to shout at me to get out. She never let me indoors during the three years I worked for her. There's nothing there now, is there?"

"No, Mr Hillier," said Gus, "our records show that the carpet in the living room has gone, and the mattress in the bedroom too. The maintenance people Mr Wakeley uses would have fixed the back door, the guttering, and anything else that's started falling off over the past five years."

"I don't know why Arthur doesn't sell it," said Don Hillier.

"Mrs Wakeley told us that the bungalow's boarded up," said Gus. "Before we drive there, do you have a torch, Mr Hillier?"

Don Hillier went back inside the house and returned with two large torches.

"Living in the countryside, it's better to prepare," he said, "street lights only exist in the town. Out here, you can still find spots where it truly is pitch black at night."

"What was Ursula like to work for?" asked Lydia when she parked outside the bungalow.

"I came here every Tuesday and Thursday and did a full day's work. Ursula paid me well for my labour. She was a particular person if you get my drift. Everything had to be right. I quickly learned how to avoid a reprimand. I listened to what she said she wanted and made sure she never had cause to complain."

"Did you know about her habit of not drawing her curtains?" asked Lydia.

"That was not something she discussed with the paid help, Miss. After three years of never arriving to find a curtain even partly drawn, I realised something was wrong straight away that morning."

"Let's wander around the grounds," said Gus. "Has it changed since you came here last?"

"This is the first time I've been near the bungalow since that day, Mr Freeman. After Arthur came out and said what he'd found, I waited for the police to arrive. They questioned me, as you would expect, and when they said I could leave, I put the ladder back in the shed, locked up, and cycled home. The frost had long gone by that time. Someone has tended to the garden, I see. They've cut back the trees at the rear of the property far more than Ursula preferred. There were more overhanging branches, and she left the brambles to run wild. They've scrubbed those out now."

"Why did Ursula keep them," asked Gus, "did she enjoy picking the blackberries?"

"She picked a few but told me I could collect whatever I needed. Ursula allowed the boundary at the back garden to grow wild, to screen those fields behind. That was where her father died. And there's a footpath crossing the field. Ramblers use it to make sure it's kept open."

"We've got a key to the shed," said Gus, "I wonder whether the maintenance firm stores any of their gear here?"

He opened the shed door, and Don took a look.

"The step ladder's still there," he said, "and the old lawnmower I used to use. They've cleared out odds and ends, half bags of fertiliser, packets of seeds. The tools Ursula's father left that I used are stacked in the corner. The cobwebs tell their own story. It isn't in use any longer."

"Do you feel up to coming indoors with us now, Mr Hillier?" asked Gus.

Don Hillier shrugged.

"I don't believe in ghosts, Mr Freeman."

Lydia felt a shiver down her spine as they stepped over the threshold. Ursula's handyman hadn't witnessed the body. He may have heard stories of the killer's actions, but Lydia had seen the photographs.

Gus walked into the living room, and his shoes echoed on the bare boards of the wooden floor. He shone Don Hillier's torch around the walls and on the floor.

"Strange, isn't it?" said Don. "Her furniture doesn't look to have moved. Why didn't Arthur remove these ornaments or even unplug her old TV?"

"There aren't any family photographs," said Lydia. "Were there any when you worked here?"

"No idea, Miss. I never came indoors. When I was up the ladder, peering in that day, I only wondered if she was alright."

"We'll check whether Arthur had items removed," said Gus. "He said he's never been back."

"Several of these ornaments are souvenirs from tourist destinations," said Lydia.

"Ursula went on foreign holidays after her mother died," said Don. "Coach trips mostly, I don't remember her mentioning that she flew anywhere, but I might be wrong. That had stopped by the time I started working for her. She told me she was too busy at the library to take a holiday."

"There's only one thing that appears to be missing from the kitchen," said Gus, who had left Don and Lydia in the living room.

"The murder weapon," said Lydia. She heard Don's intake of breath.

"Ursula didn't own a separate freezer," said Gus. "Her fridge is empty, and there's nothing in the larder."

"Her parents never moved with the times, Mr Freeman," said Don. "My mother managed perfectly well with a store cupboard in the kitchen. She relented and had a fridge when she was in her seventies. We bought fresh produce every couple of days, cooked it and ate it, then put the few scraps out for the animals. We couldn't afford to waste anything."

"A different world," said Gus. "Ursula's kitchen had its roots in the 1950s, but with a brand-new fridge."

Gus headed towards the hallway again.

"Are you familiar with the layout of these bungalows, Don?"

"Not one hundred per cent," he said, "but on this side of the house, there must be two bedrooms at the rear, the family bathroom, and then the main bedroom at the front. Who slept where heaven knows."

"We'll start at the back," said Gus.

"Good," said Lydia. Any delay in entering the front bedroom was acceptable to her.

Chapter Seven

THEY HAD LEFT the front door open, so the hallway wasn't as dark as the living room and kitchen. The back bedroom door creaked when Gus opened it.

"Blimey," said Don.

"Exactly," said Gus. "No prizes for guessing whose room this was. I half-expected to find a teenage Arthur asleep in the bed. Nobody has touched this room for decades. When was he born?"

"Thirty-three, guv," said Lydia. "Glenda told me they married two weeks after the Coronation in 1953. Matthew arrived three years later, followed by Samantha in 1958."

"What did you have on the walls in your bedroom, Don?" asked Gus.

"Wallpaper, for a start. I had a large map of the world, rather than a globe—two pictures. We couldn't afford a carpet, so it was linoleum and a mat by the bed. Even so, it felt warmer than this does. This is spartan, isn't it? No decoration at all."

"No books, magazines, or comics. Just as Glenda predicted," said Lydia. "It's like a monk's cell."

"Things changed once he left here and married," said Gus, "the house we were in an hour ago was decidedly normal. Nothing more nor less than you expect for an elderly couple these days."

"Money helps with that, guv. Perhaps Arthur wanted to leave everything he'd experienced growing up behind him."

"I think nothing's moved," said Gus. "We're seeing it as it was the day Arthur left to get married. His mother closed the door, and that was that."

"Next door will be the box room, then," said Don. "Ursula's bedroom, as she was the youngest child."

Lydia opened the door.

"What a tiny room," she said.

"Seven foot by six foot, would you say, Mr Freeman?" asked Don Hillier.

"I agree. I reckon Ursula cleared this room when her mother died," said Gus. "She moved into the room at the front by 1997. Every piece of furniture from this bedroom has gone. What does that suggest?"

"It was a mirror image of Arthur's room, guv. Sterile and with no decoration. Look at the curtains. Blue and white check. They were purely functional and drab."

"What's in those cardboard boxes?" asked Don.

"Old clothes belonging to her parents, according to our records," said Gus.

"Do you want to check, guv?" asked Lydia.

"I'll step outside if you think it's none of my business," said Don.

"Up to you," said Gus, "We're unlikely to discover anything horrific. I'd be kicking up a fuss at Salisbury nick if they hadn't been through every box searching for potential clues. If we dig deep enough into the original file back in the office, you should find an itemised inventory. It might have got lost, I suppose. It's hard to see how it could be relevant."

Lydia opened the top box. She took a pair of nitrile gloves from her pocket.

"Night clothes and underwear," she said.

"Let me help you, Miss," said Don, moving forward to lift the box to one side.

"I can manage," said Lydia, "you could take the others from the stack and put them on the floor. Gus and I can get through them quicker together."

Gus ferreted in his jacket pocket, hoping he'd remembered his gloves. He was in luck.

Boxes two, three and four contained old clothes belonging to Gideon, Elspeth and their two children. There were no toys of any description.

"They didn't even keep their baby clothes or christening gowns," said Lydia. "What about their baby teeth or the curls from their first haircut? What kind of people were they?"

Gus lifted the corner of the last box.

"This is the heaviest of the lot," he said. "I think we can guess what's in here."

He opened the lid and stood back.

"Blimey," said Don Hillier.

The first two items were Victorian family Bibles. They looked magnificent.

"They're heavy," said Lydia, "this one has to be over five kilos."

"A pressed leather exterior, gilt cartouche for the title, and gilt clasps still in perfect working order after one hundred and forty years?"

"They're full of sepia engravings and revivalist illuminations," said Lydia.

"They must be worth a fair bit," said Don Hillier. "Do you reckon this was what those burglars wanted?"

"Only if these Bibles hid gold bars inside them," said Gus.

"What's under the cloth protecting the Bibles, guv?" asked Lydia.

"More religious texts, Bible stories, hymn books. There are several certificates here for Sunday school attendance prizes awarded to Arthur and Ursula. No big surprises in there. Everything relates to the Methodist Church. Guess what? Right at the very bottom is a single photo album."

"Black and white?" asked Don Hillier.

"Dog-eared and faded, yes. It's from Gideon and Elspeth's wedding in 1930. There's nothing of the children. No birthday party, no playing in the garden. No family day out on the beach at Weymouth. Nothing."

"Arthur appeared to survive his brutal upbringing alright, guv," said Lydia. "You wouldn't say unscathed, but once he escaped their clutches, he lived a relatively normal life."

"I never knew Ursula had to endure such hardship," said Don. "It explains her strange ways."

"There's nothing more to see," said Gus. "We should leave the room as we found it. Then we'll have a quick look next door and get you back home, Don."

Two minutes later, they stood outside the front bedroom door.

"This is where it happened, is it?" asked Don.

Gus nodded.

"Don't feel obliged to come in, Don."

Gus and Lydia stepped inside.

Lydia laughed.

"I never expected that," said Gus.

"Ursula had the room decorated in the late Nineties," said Lydia. "This was the room she wanted when she was a young girl. It reminded me of my bedroom in Dundee when I was five or six years old."

Gus looked over his shoulder. Don Hillier was hovering by the front door. Gus steered Lydia further into the room so they could speak in private.

"The naked body, the knife wounds, and the blood dominated the crime scene photos. Ursula's surroundings faded into the background so much that I never imagined for one moment her bedroom was bright and colourful. She never attempted to decorate the kitchen and living room. This bedroom was Ursula's sanctuary, where she could live the life her parents denied her."

"I'm surprised she remained sane after seventy-eight years living in a time capsule," said Lydia. "Although maybe she didn't."

"We didn't check the bathroom," said Gus.

"Are you ready to go?" asked Don, "I felt a chill just now."

"You said you didn't believe in ghosts," said Gus. "We won't be a second."

Lydia opened the bathroom door.

"Back to the Fifties, guv. How can anyone manage without a shower or a heated towel rail?"

"Those Victorian Roll-Top baths are popular again," said Gus. "I wonder where the outside toilet used to be before they had this one installed?"

"At the bottom of the garden, near the trees," said Don, "It had gone when I started working here, but the concrete base still exists. There's a butt there now to collect rainwater."

"Right, that's everything," said Gus. "We'll run you back home, Don."

"Will you need to speak to me again?" he asked.

"Why? Is there something you haven't told us?"

"I'm not hiding any secrets, Mr Freeman."

"Did the detectives ever ask if you knew who might have had a grudge against Ursula?"

"They were keen to pin it on me, Mr Freeman. That fellow Kite talked to me several times. Half a dozen witnesses saw me in the Walnut Tree Inn that evening. After that, they dashed over to Ringwood to pursue the burglary aspect. Nothing ever came of it, so now you're back again. How long have you got, Mr Freeman? It might take a while if you want the names of people who Ursula annoyed. Take that footpath behind those trees. Families have lived here for generations in small towns such as Mere. In Gideon's day, everyone in town knew everyone else. There are houses around these parts now that carry a fancy price. You know the major landowner in the region, I imagine?"

"The Duchy of Cornwall," said Gus. "I picked up local knowledge working for thirty years in Salisbury, Don. Wiltshire is one of twenty-three counties in England with land governed by the estate. Edward III established it in 1337. The Gillingham estate extends into the county, but the exact boundaries aren't clear."

"Enough said. Well, over the years, there's been an influx of wealthy types. Incomers, we call them—people who come to live in an area where they didn't grow up. I'm not the type that wants to run them out of town. Live and let live, that's my motto, but some don't take kindly to folks who move here and want to change things that have been a particular way for hundreds of years."

"I can imagine Gideon stood firm against such people," said Gus.

"Ursula, too," said Don.

"Who owns the land behind the bungalow?" asked Gus.

"A chap called Hurley. He's a wealthy financier who moved out of London twenty-five years ago. He owns a seven-bedroomed house on an estate on the outskirts of Gillingham."

"Twenty-five years?" said Lydia. "Do the locals still call him an incomer?"

"He's got another generation to go before he becomes one of us, Miss. Hurley earns more in bonuses every week than you do in a year," said Don. "His estate is far enough away not to see the housing estate he wanted to get built on that land. He bought it years ago with an eye on future development. However, there was something in his way."

"The footpath that runs across the land close to Ursula's bungalow," said Gus.

"Ursula said her piece in town frequently when the initial land purchase went through. You know how these things go, Mr Freeman. Unless you keep your eyes peeled, the required notice of intent slips past you in a local news-paper, and the deed gets done. Ursula accused the Council of taking a back-hander from this Hurley chap and failing to block yet another assault on the green belt. Mere is a tiny town with half a dozen villages nearby. If hundreds of houses went up in areas like Shaftesbury Road, the town would lose its identity in a decade. Hurley saw an opportu-nity to cash in when the land was cheap. Five years after this affair blew up, James Bendick got involved. He bought land on the other side of the road."

"What, Bendick, the shipping magnate? Does he live around here?" asked Gus.

"Bendick has homes in London and Monte Carlo, Mr Freeman, but he's got a young wife these days, and she lives in a listed building on Castle Hill. His land doesn't have a right-of-way to concern him. But Ursula saw the danger that the purchase could pose. She wasn't shy in letting people know how she felt. If one or the other of them got a foot in the door, then more and more developers would jump on the bandwagon."

Gus shared a glance with Lydia. Now they were getting somewhere. Gus wondered why Jefferson and Kite hadn't explored this angle.

"Together with the Ramblers Association, a campaigner argued that the track crossing the farmland Gideon Wakeley had worked on throughout his life became a public right of way in 1841. On that basis, the track should get shown as a public bridleway on the area's definitive map. A government inspector presided over a public inquiry, and the campaigner didn't persuade him and the local authority to agree with his view. As soon as that became public knowledge, Ursula Wakeley told anyone who would listen that Hurley had the local authority in his pocket."

"What reason did they give?" asked Gus.

"Hurley's legal counsel reckoned that in 1841, the commissioners only had the power to create private, rather than public, rights of way," said Don. "He said they had misinterpreted the wording of the original Act of Parliament from 1801."

"Couldn't they have argued that even though the decision was a technical error, the passage of time and long-established practice of using the footpath should be considered?"

"Oh, they did, but it didn't make a difference."

"It seems complicated to me," said Lydia. "Isn't it a case of 'Not In My Back Yard' with people like Ursula wanting her remote bungalow to stay as it had been for generations?"

"When did this kerfuffle take place, Don?" asked Gus.

"I was still working back then. Let me think. Hurley bought his place in the early 1990s. Bendick wasn't far behind him. You need to check when it was exactly, but Hurley purchased the land within a year or two of moving into the district."

"Before or after Ursula's mother died?" asked Gus.

"I'm not sure," said Don, "But Bendick made his move five years later. Everything's gone quiet since Ursula's murder. She's not around to stir things up, but there's been less talk of housing development, and that footpath is still in use. The Ramblers' Association makes sure of that."

"Many thanks, Don," said Gus. "We'll let you get on.

"You know where I am if you need me. I'll have my torch back if you please. I'll likely need it before you."

"I hadn't forgotten," said Gus, handing it over.

Don Hillier walked up the pathway to his house. Lydia returned to the Mini.

"We'd better get back to the office," said Gus, "Neil and Blessing will wonder what's taken us so long."

WHILE GUS and Lydia conducted interviews with Arthur and Glenda Wakeley and Don Hillier, Neil Davis and Blessing Umeh visited the town and its library. Neil parked the car in Castle Street, and they walked around the centre for a few minutes.

"How are you settling in with Suzie Ferris's parents?" asked Neil.

"They are very kind," said Blessing, "I've not seen Suzie much yet. She wasn't at home when I arrived on Sunday."

"Suzie would have been in Urchfont with Gus," said Neil.

"Did they meet about work?" asked Blessing.

"How well do you know our team members, Blessing?"

"Very little. I realise you are a close unit. Even though you've only worked together for a few months, there are a lot of moments you have shared."

"Well, Gus has been seeing Suzie for several weeks. I'm not sure how far the relationship had progressed before she got kidnapped, but it ratcheted up several notches after that. Luke reckons you couldn't have got a cigarette paper between them in the car on the way home from Leek Wotton."

"That's close, isn't it? I don't know what cigarette paper is, but it sounds like they are lovers."

"Oh, they're close, alright," said Neil. "You won't see much of Suzie at the weekend, except for when she goes riding. She stables her horse at the farm. Do you ride, Blessing?"

"No, I don't think big animals like me. I love cats, though."

"As for the others, you know about Luke and Nicky. They got engaged while we had our holiday."

"They are lucky to live in this country," said Blessing. "My father has views on people like Luke and Nicky that are not the same as mine. I shall have to watch every word I say when I'm with my parents. I must convince them Nicky is a girl."

"Your father is strict with you, I imagine?"

"My father gives the impression that he is more liberal than many of his fellow countrymen, and in some areas, he is, but with me, he always wants to check that I'm mixing with the right people. He doesn't want me to disgrace the family."

"My parents were never strict with me," said Neil. "I could twist my Mum around my little finger. But, on the other hand, Dad was always working, so my mother raised me."

"Your father died, didn't he?" asked Blessing.

"Not long before Suzie got kidnapped, yes. It was a terrible time. Melody told me she was pregnant, and then everything went pear-shaped. The stress of it brought on her miscarriage. We've struggled to overcome it, but we're getting there now."

"That must have been a horrid time for you both."

"That leaves Lydia and Alex, who gelled as soon as they met. Looking at Alex this week, he's close to recovering from his motorcycle injuries. That accident was two years ago now. Alex was lucky to survive. This last month has been a setback, but Lydia and Alex's family have got him through."

"When I first met Lydia, she impressed me with how she handled herself. She's so confident and knowledgeable. It was Lydia who inspired me to ask to move south. If I could work with the Crime Review Team and become as confident as Lydia, I would make my father proud."

"What do you make of the town of Mere?" asked Neil.

"It's little more than a large village," said Blessing. "The people are well-off, everyone drives a car, and there are more senior citizens than where I lived."

"I wasn't thinking of the demographics. What about the beauty of the place? See that sign over there?"

"The one with the arrow pointing towards the Monarch's Way. Is that a bar?"

"No, Blessing, it's another small part of this country's history. A footpath runs for over six hundred miles, tracing the escape route taken by King Charles II after his defeat at the Battle of Worcester in 1651. He travelled to Bristol, Yeovil, and across the country to Shoreham in West Sussex. After crossing the river Stour, he reached Zeals, two-and-a-half miles away. He passed through Mere on his way to Cleeve Hill."

"It was a very winding route to take," said Blessing.

"Everywhere he turned, King Charles found his path blocked by his enemies. It took another month after he came here before he got a boat to carry him to France and safety."

"I have so much to learn," said Blessing, "and I was born here."

"They don't teach History like they used to," said Neil. "But I told you that story about a convoluted trip to explain what can happen on a cold case. When we heard the bare bones of this murder, Gus told us the original investigation concentrated on the burglary aspect. Now we're visiting the library. We could have several more twists and turns before we know we're on the right road."

When they reached the door, Blessing pointed to an advert.

"I can't imagine our victim favouring that," she said.

"A toddler bounce and rhymes session? No, she believed it was time for quiet libraries to come back. Mere is a town where the library is another facility that's very much a community hub. It's the modern way, I suppose."

"I think you need balance in everything," said Blessing. "If this building is to be useful to everyone in society, it needs rules to limit noise levels and the use of mobile phones and ban the consumption of food and drink. There's a time and place."

"Let's limit our noise levels, seek out Monica Butterworth and ask her to find a place where we can talk freely."

Several heads turned as they entered. Neil had no idea whether this was a good crowd or not. Finally, a white-haired lady approached them, wearing a quizzical expression.

"Are you lost, dears?" she asked.

Neil thought that was rich. Her accent came from the north of the borders. How did she get here in the depths of the Wiltshire countryside?

"My name is Detective Sergeant Davis. My colleague is Detective Constable Umeh. We're with the Crime Review Team from Wiltshire Police. I'm sure you remember the murder of your colleague five years ago. We're taking a fresh look for Ursula Wakeley's killer."

"Oh, my word, what do you want to know?"

"Can we go somewhere we won't disturb your customers?"

"There's a room at the back, dear. We won't disturb anyone there."

Neil and Blessing followed Monica Butterworth to a glorified storeroom at the back of the building.

"It's not ideal," she said, "but we're outgrowing the space available. People value libraries; they're an asset to communities. A calm, neutral space where anyone can access information for work or leisure."

"I thought fewer people used libraries than in the past," said Blessing. "So much is available online these days."

"Despite that, a third of adults visit a library annually.

That's worth protecting. We're not just for the printed word; our telecentre is next door."

"What's that when it's at home?" asked Neil, looking puzzled.

"A room filled with computer equipment, usually in rural areas," said Blessing, "for the shared use of the local population."

"When was that installed?" asked Neil.

"In the early Nineties," replied Monica, "we've had several upgrades since, although our wi-fi signal can be troublesome. Download speeds are too slow for many of our more ardent members."

"How did Ursula Wakeley respond to the significant changes she found when she returned to work?" asked Neil.

"Detective, it devastated us to hear of Ursula's death, but she could be a trial sometimes."

Neil realised that this would not be a straightforward conversation.

"When did you start work here, Mrs Butterworth," asked Blessing.

"Monday, the first of August, in 1988," Monica replied. "Ursula came here within an hour of the library opening that morning. She came every Monday, Wednesday, and Friday morning. I longed for Tuesday and Thursday to arrive. I only worked one Saturday in four, but Ursula never missed a Saturday afternoon until the day she died. She still visited three times in the week and on Saturday afternoon after she stopped working here in 2010."

"What was she like as a colleague?" asked Neil.

"Ursula was particular about behaviour. She believed that children should be seen and not heard. Ursula wanted the library to turn the clock back forty years to the sterile environment that existed here when she left school. There were things at which she excelled. Ursula knew where every book was, and when it was out on loan, she could tell someone exactly when it should return. We have systems to do that for us. It's unnecessary to carry such detail in your head. But Ursula didn't change her ways. We only needed to have one mistake where the digital record was wrong because of a clerical error, and I could hear the 'tut' from the other side of the library. She used to say it would never have happened in my day."

"What possessed you to take her back after her mother died?" asked Neil.

"Ursula would continue coming here whatever we did. When a staff member left to have a baby and decided not to return to work, we thought it was a case of better the devil, you know. Ursula knew her stuff; there was little need for a tuition period."

"Surely, Ursula wasn't in favour of computers in the library?" asked Blessing.

Monica Butterworth giggled. It caught Neil by surprise. The Scottish lady in front of him was seventy if she was a day, but the giggle made her sound like a sixteen-year-old schoolgirl.

"I thought we'd have the devil of a job with her," she said, "but I found her next door on many an occasion."

"There was nothing in the files we received to suggest Ursula ever attended any computer courses," said Neil, "was she self-taught?"

"I don't know, and what was it to do with me? She handled a different library section and left the younger staff members to answer any computer queries people might have had."

"How did Ursula get on with the wide age range of users you get here?" asked Neil.

Monica Butterworth sat back in her chair. Neil had seen this look before.

Monica was debating whether to reveal something damaging concerning Ursula. He'd often experienced witnesses battling with their conscience.

"It's always best, to tell the truth," said Blessing. "We'll find out in the end."

Blimey, thought Neil. She's a quick learner. Well played, Blessing.

Monica came to a decision. She stood up and went to a cupboard.

"I put this away as soon as we heard the news of her death," she said. "Perhaps I should have told the police back then, but what happened to Ursula was awful. I thought it would be cruel to add this into the mix."

Neil and Blessing stared at the steel ruler Monica laid on the table.

"This belonged to Ursula?" asked Neil.

"It did when she first worked here. She had a habit of rapping the knuckles of people she caught doing something which in her eyes was inexcusable."

"How did she get away with it? You can't do that now," said Blessing.

"Her managers challenged her, of course, but she shrugged her shoulders and said that just because they permitted unacceptable behaviour, it didn't mean that she should. We told her things had altered drastically in that regard when she returned to work. No wonder that standards have dropped, Ursula would say. She said that discipline didn't do her any harm. Spare the rod and spoil the child."

"How did it work out when Ursula came back?" asked Neil.

"Ursula carried the ruler with her if children were getting restless and the noise levels rose. If it continued, she hit the table beside the prime culprit—just one sharp whack. After the first couple of occasions, the message sunk in. The kids stopped coming in when Ursula was working, or they toed the line. Because she was a spinster, we thought she wasn't used to being around children, so we kept her out of their way wherever possible. In the afternoons, there were fresh problems. We get the unemployed who drift indoors to keep warm during the winter. They've been in town for a lunchtime drink or two. If Ursula caught them nodding off, she'd smack the table to wake them up and tell them they should get home to their beds. The library was a place of learning, not a doss house."

"Did Ursula threaten other adults?" asked Blessing.

"There was one occasion," said Monica, who looked uncomfortable. "Ursula was patrolling a quiet corner where a man was reading a book. I imagine it was, shall we say, stimulating. She caught him masturbating and used the steel ruler. From the noise he made, it wasn't his knuckles she struck. We never received a complaint that time, though."

"Any more instances you can recall?" asked Neil.

"The teenagers got the most attention," said Monica, "both in the main reading area and computer room. We discourage mobile phone use, but kids today can't function without them. It wasn't an issue when Ursula started back with us in 1996, but as time passed, more and more kids were with phones. It was only a matter of time before Ursula lost her temper with someone."

"Anyone in particular?" asked Blessing.

Monica gave a wry smile.

"Anyone between the age of thirteen and eighteen. Ursula wasn't fussy. Her reprimands were legendary. I lost count of the children who suffered."

"Were there many complaints?" asked Neil. "Did any parents come here looking for blood?"

"Can you remember when you were that age, Detective Davis? Did you run home and tell your parents someone told you off for doing something wrong? Even if it wasn't against the law, it was liable to ruin the enjoyment of others who visited the library?"

"I can imagine the older teenagers gave as good as they got," said Neil. "Did anyone threaten Ursula?"

"You must remember that we cover opening hours in shifts, Detective. I couldn't be here all day, every day. I heard that there were stand-up rows with youngsters, and the language was colourful. People can be cruel. Ursula got called names because she wasn't married, didn't have children, and lived alone. She got called a dried-up, lonely old witch at least once a week, which was one of the less cutting comments. It would be best if you talked to more people in town to understand Ursula better. She had plenty to say about everyone she met, and often it wasn't complimentary."

"Is it fair to say you didn't like her?" asked Blessing.

"I got on with Ursula as well as anyone could in the circumstances," said Monica. "I appreciated that her life had been tough. She was intelligent; her knowledge of certain writers was greater than mine, and I enjoyed our lively discussions. Ursula would have made a wonderful English teacher if only her parents had allowed her to blossom. But instead, her religious upbringing made her difficult to like. As soon as someone did something she disapproved of, out came a passage from the Bible. You know how cruel and hurtful those Old Testament prophets were."

Neil struggled to remember the names of any he read at school.

Blessing held her tongue.

"What information do people need to provide when they join the library?" asked Neil.

"We have names and addresses for everyone with a library card," said Monica. "If people want us to advise them when a book they've ordered is available, we can use a phone number or email to contact them if they provide it. We don't use the data they supply for any other purpose if that's what you're asking."

"So, could I use the library without a card?" asked Neil.

"You can sign in as a day visitor," said Monica. "No matter what you access, whether it's a book you borrow or something you download online, that information is sacrosanct. No library ever reveals that information."

"I wasn't concerned with what people read," said Neil. "I wondered whether Ursula's killer sat in the library or next door in the computer room, and something happened that led to her murder."

"Surely not?" said Monica. "Ursula was an awkward customer who upset people, but even the youngsters she chastised wouldn't want to kill her."

"Who else should we interview?" asked Blessing.

"Ursula went to the same store to do her weekly shop on Saturdays. They would have stories to tell. The café in the town centre was another of her favourite spots. The owner there will remember her."

"Many thanks, Mrs Butterworth," said Neil. "We may

return if our boss thinks we need access to your old card records."

"I'll speak to my superiors at the Council," said Monica. "They may object, but if it's going to help find Ursula's killer, I'm sure we can work something out."

Neil and Blessing left the library and walked into the town centre.

Chapter Eight

"URSULA WAKELEY COULD BE AN UNPLEASANT WOMAN," said Blessing. "Yet Monica Butterworth still found it in her heart to defend her. I can't imagine my English teacher being horrid to everyone she met and discussing the Lake poets in glowing terms."

"The more we learn, the more I realise that Ursula was a troubled soul, Blessing," said Neil. "I wonder what Gus and Lydia have uncovered? Ah well, let's visit the café first. I'll stand you a cup of coffee, and we can grill the owner."

"Can I have a toasted teacake, too?" asked Blessing.

"Don't push it just because you're the new kid," said Neil.

The café was a bustling little place, ideally situated on the corner of the street opposite the town's major row of shops—Neil and Blessing sat and people-watched as they waited to get served.

"I wonder how many of these pedestrians Ursula insulted?" said Nel.

"Shall we ask them?" asked Blessing.

"Not until we've had something to eat and drink."

There were two members of staff hard at work. The younger girl looked across at Neil more than once. Then, as Neil thought she was heading their way, someone caught her attention at a nearby table.

"What can I get you?" said a voice. The older lady, who looked like she was in charge, had crept up behind him.

Blessing gave the order, and Neil waited until the lady returned with their coffees and teacakes.

"Are you the owner?" he said.

"That's me. I'm Jenny Medcroft. What's the matter?"

"Nothing," said Neil, "I'm sure it will taste wonderful. We're with Wiltshire Police."

Neil and Blessing showed Jenny their warrant cards. She sat on a spare chair next to Neil.

"How can I help?" she asked.

"Do you remember the murder of a lady called Ursula Wakeley around five years ago?"

"I do. Ursula was a regular in here. Sometimes she was alone, but other times she met up with her brother and his wife. Why?"

"Were there occasions you thought of asking her to leave or banning her?"

"Every week, dear. Ursula could be a nightmare. It was just her way. There was no harm in her, or at least I never thought so. You know those people that suddenly blurt something out; they can't control themselves. Ursula was like that."

"Tourette's," said Blessing Umeh.

"That's it, dear. I couldn't remember the name. Ursula came in here, ordered a pot of tea and always sat in the same spot by the window. She watched the people walking past the window, and if she saw someone she didn't like the look of, she'd say something, you know?"

"Can you remember what she might say?" asked Neil.

"Not the exact phrases, but something related to repenting your sins."

"*Repent and turn again, that your sins may be blotted out,*" said Blessing.

"Do you know, that *was* one of her sayings," said Jenny. "Ursula didn't make a fuss; there was no waving her arms or banging on the window. Instead, calm as you like, she'd sit there, stirring her tea and say things as you did."

"Did anyone argue with Ursula while she was in your café?" asked Neil.

"Not that I can remember, dear. Becky might recall. Let me give her a shout. Becky?"

A third staff member emerged from behind the counter. The woman resembled Jenny.

"Becky Medcroft?" asked Neil taking a punt.

"Becky Burden, now, I'm married," the woman replied.

"These detectives were asking about Ursula, Becky. Can you remember her arguing with anyone in the café?"

"There were those students that gave her grief one Saturday afternoon," said Becky. "They stood outside the window right where she always sat and started kissing. They did it deliberately because they knew it annoyed her. We should discourage public displays of affection in public. That was one of her favourite expressions when she saw couples getting too close in here. Those kids never came to this café, though. We weren't posh enough for them. Everyone in this café knew what Ursula was like. I won't say that nobody took offence, but if you think someone killed her over a few words, then I can't see it, I'm afraid."

"Can you remember any of the words she used, Becky?" asked Neil.

"The Lord disciplines those he loves," said Becky. "I remember that one because it didn't sound right."

"God is a parent," said Blessing. "You do not punish your child because you hate them and want to see them suffer. Most parents punish their children for their own good. So they can learn from the consequences of their actions and never repeat them."

"Well, I never punish my kids," said Becky, returning behind the counter to the kitchen.

"Blessing, am I right in thinking Ursula knew more about discipline than most?" asked Neil.

"We should tell Gus Freeman this," she replied. "Perhaps her parents were strict with her. If she suffered as a child, that influenced how she saw the world as she grew older. It could explain her outbursts. My teacake is delicious, Mrs Medcroft. Thank you."

"You're welcome, I'm sure," said Jenny Medcroft. "I must get on; customers are waiting. Was there anything else you needed to ask?"

"I think that's enough for now, Mrs Medcroft," said Neil. "We're off to the supermarket next."

When Blessing and Neil got outside, he walked along the pavement and stopped where Ursula used to sit. Blessing joined him and looked around.

"It was a good vantage point to see most of the Square over there," he said. "Ursula didn't miss much, did she?"

"I wonder what type of person made her shout out," said Blessing. "It sounds like she knew everyone's weakness, doesn't it? The drinkers, gamblers, and idlers passed by her window. The café we just left and the library. They are both good places to overhear gossip or catch people meeting secretly. Ursula was a commentator on the sins of the modern world."

"That's one way to describe it," said Neil. "I don't know whether Gus agrees."

"Mr Freeman is not a church-going man, so I've heard," said Blessing.

"Gus has a particular view on religion, Blessing. I think that's fair to say."

"Who do you think was kissing by this window that day, Neil?"

"Two students, Becky Burden, said. They will have left school, disappeared to a dark corner of the world to find themselves or married, probably to different people, by now. Let's see what they have to say in the Co-op."

Thirty minutes later, they returned to the car park in Castle Street.

"They have a high staff turnover, don't they?" said Blessing.

"The older bloke in the butchery department remembered Ursula," said Neil. "He thought she was strait-laced and severe. Ursula was typical of women of his mother's era who checked every rasher of bacon and sausage. Meat was still rationed until 1954. Unscrupulous butchers tried to fob people off with inferior quality cuts or wrap five sausages in a bundle instead of six. Ursula reminded that butcher of those times. She wanted everything just so. The store manager retired last year, and the delivery drivers have changed. The butcher remembered the fuss Ursula made when she finished gathering her order every Saturday. Her shopping had to arrive at a precise time. Ursula stood on the doorstep, waiting for the van to stop outside her door."

"Why didn't her brother help?" asked Blessing.

"They don't appear to have got on," said Neil. "Gus will tell us more when we get back to the office, no doubt."

"Do you think we've made progress, Neil?"

"We learned about the steel ruler, the relic from Ursula's early days at the library. Spare the rod, and spoil the child. Discipline keeps cropping up, doesn't it? It has to be significant. I was interested in what use Ursula made of the tele-centre thing. It doesn't feel right. I'm not saying she was a technophobe, but she never had a mobile phone, tablet or laptop at home. What did she access while she was in there?"

"Ursula was a troubled soul," said Blessing, "we keep coming back to that. But, perhaps she was a simple soul, too, and played Solitaire or Free Cell. There must be plenty of downtime for a librarian in a small town."

"Would there be evidence of what she used the computers for?" asked Neil, "Surely she had to log on? What was her username, I wonder?"

"You heard what Monica Butterworth said. Libraries have a strict code of ethics. We'll meet resistance unless we have evidence that Ursula committed a crime. How would we discover her password, anyway? The library has had several upgrades to its systems too. Would Ursula's activity still be accessible after five years? It might be a blind alley, Neil."

"You're probably right, Blessing. I'll tell you what, though; we could check a list of names of library card-holders against their social media accounts—especially the younger ones. Someone like Ursula would be certain to get a mention when they were chatting. We might get an idea of who wanted her stopped."

"You might have hit on a great idea there, Neil," said Blessing.

"I have them now and then," said Neil.

They returned to the Old Police Station office to discover they had arrived before Gus and Lydia.

"How did you two get on?" asked Luke.

"We had coffee and toasted teacakes," said Neil.

"Lucky dogs," said Luke, "I made several fruitless phone calls. However, the appointments for tomorrow at the church and with the shopkeepers in Ringwood are confirmed. Getting hold of Fabian Kite has proved tricky. Mel Jefferson is calling back this afternoon around five o'clock. Typical, I have to stay late. Nicky and I were playing squash tonight. Never mind, fill me in on what you learned about Ursula, the sinister spinster."

"I think that's unfair, Luke," said Blessing. "The character we're uncovering divided opinion. One person told us she was eccentric but meant no harm. Another wrestled with her conscience before admitting Ursula used to hit children who misbehaved with a steel ruler when she worked there before her father died. Ursula had a brilliant mind and loved discussing literature with her colleague. Those who knew her for decades accepted her behaviour more readily than youngsters who came into contact with her."

"Yeah," said Neil, "Blessing's right. Unfortunately, we only have a smattering of information in the murder file to use. Gus wanted us to discover what this woman did to make someone not only want to kill her but to torture her and mutilate her body after death. Ursula Wakeley might have annoyed people with her outbursts, but was that enough to trigger an attack as vicious and bloody as the one in those pictures on the wall? I can't see it."

"You know what that means?" said Luke.

"We already knew we weren't dealing with a robbery

that went wrong as Jefferson and Kite believed," said Neil. "Now it feels less like a murder in response to things Ursula said or did."

"If Gus is right and there was an accomplice," said Blessing, "then we're looking for a pair of thrill-seeking killers."

"We won't have long to wait to hear how they got on," said Luke, "someone just called the lift."

Gus and Lydia arrived within a minute.

"Good, you're back," said Gus, "we've had a very productive morning. I hope you three did too. Before we debrief, I suggest we update our reports in the Freeman Files."

Gus completed his task and looked around the office. Everyone was busy except Luke.

"Luke," he said, "can you give me a list of people and times for tomorrow's interviews, please? I want to allocate resources. That should give the others time to finish."

Luke took the schedule to Gus's desk and placed it in front of him.

"Jefferson is ringing me later today. Kite is abroad, somewhere in Europe, but he's not answering any phone calls or emails. Ormrod and Dillon, the Ringwood shop-keepers, are available at two o'clock and three o'clock tomorrow afternoon, in that order. The Methodist minister, Horace Plant, can see us at eleven tomorrow morning. I've put Matthew Wakeley on standby for one o'clock. He can give us thirty minutes of his lunch break if you think we need to talk to him."

"Thanks, Luke. I want to talk to Mr Plant. Religion played a huge part in Ursula's parents' lives and influenced her greatly, even after their deaths. You and Neil could drive out to Ringwood tomorrow afternoon. I'll ask one of the girls to chat with Matthew Wakeley. He was on the periphery of things, the same as his sister. Samantha hasn't lived in the district for years. I reckon we'll only get background information and confirmation of facts the four of us gathered today. Right, is everybody ready?"

"Yes, guv," came the reply.

"You can dig into the detail later. But a quick summary of what Lydia and I discovered was as follows. Gideon Wakeley disciplined Arthur and Ursula with a switch throughout their childhood. The inside of the bungalow has remained untouched since the murder, apart from the clean-up operation carried out by Jefferson's crew. Every room in the bungalow, bar one, is a shrine to the Fifties. It's spartan, utilitarian, call it what you wish, but it wasn't a warm house, no matter how big a fire they had in the living room. Don Hillier mentioned a footpath dispute that has rumbled on for twenty-odd years. A wealthy financier who thought he could make a fortune when house-building became a priority bought the field behind the bungalow where Gideon Wakeley worked and died. So far, the footpath has remained open. Ursula was vocal in her opposition to its removal. It surprised us that Ursula's bedroom was a riot of colour. It was Nineties kitsch, I suppose, and as big a contrast to the rest of the home as you could get. Neil, what did you find out?"

"Monica Butterworth showed us a steel ruler Ursula threatened children with when she worked there between 1996 and 2010. There was no evidence to suggest she struck a child. Ursula was a stickler for behaviour in the library and adhering to the systems in place. Ursula wasn't keen on noisy teenagers and feckless adults who used the library for a quiet, warm spot to wait before returning to the pub. There's a separate room filled with computers for the public to use. According to Mrs Butterworth, Ursula spent time there, and the older lady thought people judged Ursula unfairly. She found conversations with Ursula on literature stimulating. Ursula wasn't miserable and rude all the time."

"The café manager told us that Ursula was a regular," said Blessing. "Her daughter mentioned a teenage couple kissing outside the window. They were goading Ursula, looking for a reaction. Both women in the café thought Ursula was odd, with the comments she aimed at passers-by, but there was no actual harm in what she said. Many super-market staff have left since 2013, but a man confirmed that Ursula was strict about when her shopping got delivered. She checked every item on her list to see it was as she had ordered."

"Did you come up with any potential suspects?" asked Gus.

"No more than you did by the sound of it, guv," said Neil. "I'd want to get hold of a list of those people with library cards around the time of the murder. Then, we could get the Hub to tell us whether any offenders were on the list. Then, I'd check social media accounts to search for hate speech. That might be our quickest route to a potential suspect."

"We might have a problem with that," said Gus, "on the other hand, we've got the 2011 Census to fall back on. Mere is a small town. It would take us longer, but we could throw everyone into the mix to start with whether or not they had a library card."

"That's an idea, and we wouldn't upset Monica Butter-worth then. I overheard you mention the visit to the Methodist minister, guv," said Neil. "I reckon you should take Blessing with you. She could be a big help."

"I plan to spend time with each of you where practical,"

said Gus, "the ACC might ask me for performance appraisals one day, and I'd hate to say I hadn't seen you in action. So, okay, Blessing, you're with me tomorrow. We won't need to leave here until ten, so Neil can collect you from the farm."

"Do you need to call the Ferris's, Blessing?" asked Luke, "I can't run you home at five tonight if I'm waiting for that call from South Africa."

"I don't mind waiting," said Blessing, "I don't have plans until later. My mother's calling to hear how I'm settling in."

"No problem, Luke," said Gus. "I'll take Blessing home tonight."

"Why stick with the same schedule of interviews, guv," asked Lydia, "after what we saw today?"

"What would you change, Lydia?"

"I can't see what Jefferson or Kite can offer. They got it wrong. The robbery was to throw them off the scent, and they fell for it."

"So, you wouldn't talk to them? What if Mel Jefferson tells Luke something that wasn't in the murder file? It wouldn't be the first time an officer under pressure forgot to log a sentence from a conversation or record a feeling that a witness was worth a second look. It shouldn't happen, but it does. How about Ormrod and Dillon? Why bother asking them about the jewellery? It was irrelevant. Who's to say the girl was one of the two people in the bungalow that night? The lad outside may have been her brother or a boyfriend. He might be the killer, and even five years after the event, Ormrod or Dillon could remember something trivial that links to a detail we find when trawling through those social media accounts. The devil is in the detail, Lydia. So, nothing gets ruled out until we've checked every eventuality."

"Got it, guv. Sorry."

"Does anyone else have a problem with the schedule we're following?" asked Gus.

Neil looked across to the desk where Blessing Umeh sat.

"We had a conversation before you got back, guv. Blessing wondered whether we were looking for a pair of thrill-seekers."

Gus looked at the crime scene photos.

"I won't discount the robbery element until I've heard everything from the detectives and the jewellery shop owners. Maybe I'm ultra-cautious, but better safe than sorry. I can't discount the revenge motive either until I have every hurtful comment Ursula passed and who suffered as a result. You mentioned a computer room, Neil."

"A telecentre, guv," said Neil, "it's a community resource within the library."

"Ursula never possessed a mobile phone, tablet, or laptop. I get by with what I've picked up over the past twenty years. I've had no formal training. Check whether Ursula received any. If not, then what was she able to do in that room? As for Blessing's idea, the thrill-seeker is one of the four classifications of the serial killer, isn't it? I thought we established that nothing remotely similar to Ursula Wakeley's killing took place in the region before or since 2013. Therefore, unless we find more bodies, we're not dealing with a serial killer."

Gus spent the rest of the afternoon studying those gory images and wondering whether he was right.

At five o'clock, everyone, bar Luke cleared their desks and headed for the lift.

"Good luck, Luke," said Gus. "Say hello to Mel for me. I hope he remembers something vital. At least we're not paying for the call."

Neil and Lydia were soon in their cars and heading out of the car park. Blessing sat in the passenger seat of the Focus.

"My father used to have a car like this," she said.

"I keep telling everyone. It's a classic," said Gus.

"He got rid of his after a month. The passenger-side window kept dropping without warning. It frightened my mother."

Gus decided to drive and forget conversation for a while.

They were halfway to the farm when Blessing spoke.

"I thought you wanted to reprimand me," she said. "I wondered what I did wrong."

"Reprimand you? Why on earth made you think that? I offered to run you home because that's what we do. We're a team. I wouldn't dream of leaving you outside the Old Police Station, wondering where you could catch a bus or get a taxi. The others will always help too. Have you heard from the garage yet?"

"No news is good news," said Blessing.

"Not always, but I'd stick with that for now. How are you settling in with John and Jackie?"

"I have no complaints. My bedroom is a touch masculine in décor, but it was Suzie's brother's room. The sounds in the farmyard wake me up earlier than I'm used to, but at least I'll never be late for work. I have seen little of Suzie, but her mother and father have made me most welcome."

"They've made me welcome too," said Gus, "which I thought might have been difficult, given that John and I are much the same age."

"Will you get married?" asked Blessing.

"That's a rather direct question," said Gus.

"I'm sorry," said Blessing, "I must get ready to explain

your relationship to my parents. They are coming to visit at the weekend. If Suzie's name cropped up in conversation, I want to avoid my father thinking you are living in sin, do you understand?"

"The subject of marriage has never come up in any conversation I've had with Suzie or her parents," said Gus. "We are not living together, although that situation could change. Does that offend you?"

"Not me, guv," said Blessing, "live and let live, I say. If the situation changes, I will need to watch what I say in front of my father. The same as when I speak about Luke and Nicky."

Blessing sat, wringing her hands in her lap.

"It will get complicated. I know it," said Blessing.

"That's religion for you, Blessing," said Gus. "I don't suffer these moral dilemmas. Did you get these issues back in Royal Leamington Spa? Surely someone on Andy Carlton's squad was less than perfect?"

"Only me," said Blessing.

Gus wanted to laugh but held it in. They had reached the gateway to the farm.

When he pulled up outside the farmhouse door, John Ferris strode across the yard from the nearby barn.

"Things are looking up, Blessing," he said, "the boss is bringing you home on your second day. Hello, Gus, long time no see."

"Hello, John," said Gus. "Blame Suzie. She can't stop driving over to my place. It's weeks since we came over for a meal."

"Get off with you. Jackie needed to keep busy that night while we waited for you to bring her home from Leek Wotton. Cooking was Jackie's way of taking her mind off what might have happened."

"Regardless of when it was and why It's high time I showed my face here. Perhaps we could drop by on Sunday afternoon?"

"That's when my parents are coming," said Blessing.

"Perfect timing then," said Gus, "you'll have less to worry about."

John shrugged his shoulders. Whatever that meant didn't bother him.

"Jackie will kill me if I let you disappear without coming in and having a word."

"I insist on coming in," said Gus. "I have to check that the food is up to the standard that Blessing's father expects. A taste test might be necessary."

"If you can hang on twenty minutes, Suzie will be back from Swindon, and we can test it together."

Blessing slipped away to her room above the kitchen. She wanted to shower and change before dinner. She needed to think about how she explained things to her mother when she called. My boss ran me home from work. He stayed for dinner and is still here, talking with his lover's parents.

What could she possibly object to in that?

Chapter Nine

Wednesday, 4 July 2018

GUS WAS STILL THINKING about the thrill-seekers when he got out of bed in the morning. Could Blessing be right? If only they had the tiniest clue about who broke into the bungalow that night. Perhaps something would come from today's meetings.

When Suzie returned from Gablecross last evening, she was tired and stressed. Working with Gareth Francis would tax the mildest-mannered person. It surprised Suzie to find Gus sitting in her parent's kitchen, drinking a coffee, and chatting amicably with her mother. Gus couldn't understand why. Bert Penman had told everyone within earshot that Suzie was his intended. The rumour mill in villages such as Urchfont and Worton was well-oiled. Jackie Ferris would have heard within the hour. Whether she passed that message on to her husband, John, was another matter.

Blessing Umeh had arrived downstairs looking refreshed minutes after Suzie came indoors, and the penny dropped.

Gus had driven the new DC home because one of the boys got delayed at work. Whatever the reason for his unexpected presence, Suzie seemed content. The wine helped, but Gus was driving and limited himself to one glass of beer.

Gus couldn't imagine what Blessing made of the conversation that Suzie and her parents continued over the meal the five of them shared. Several farming terms were foreign even to his ears, but John Ferris still smiled at the end. So it couldn't have been too financially damaging.

When Blessing's mobile rang at eight o'clock, she announced that her mother was calling and went upstairs. Suzie and Gus walked around the farmyard, and she tended to her horse in the stable. When Gus drove home at nine, he felt guilty about leaving her behind.

The drive through Devizes this morning was uneventful for a change, and with Alex Hardy giving him a wave as he headed towards London Road, Gus was confident parking wouldn't be a problem when he reached the Old Police Station. Unfortunately, he still hadn't spoken to Geoff Mercer about fixing that issue. How many mental notes was that now?

Upstairs in the office, Neil and Blessing were already at work. Lydia was in the restroom. As Gus fired up his computer, he heard the lift return to the ground floor. Luke was on his way.

The lift doors opened and in breezed Luke.

"Good morning, everyone," he cried. "What a beautiful morning."

"Too much, Luke, but nice try," said Gus. "Tell me how awful the phone call was last night. You got nothing from Mel Jefferson, did you?"

"It surprised Jefferson that you came out of retirement,

guv," said Luke. "He thought you had more sense. I reminded him how successful you had been since setting up this team. Jefferson thought it was just as well you had early success because this case would be your downfall. Ursula never spoke with more than a dozen people in the last twenty years of her life. Her mother dominated every waking minute of her life between her father's death and that of her mother in '96. After that, it was Arthur, Glenda, Don Hillier, Monica Butterworth, a handful of people at the new Methodist Church building and the staff at the café and supermarket. Ursula talked about a hundred people and complained about a hundred more in the library, but a conversation was not on the list of her priorities. Ursula was a recluse for most of the week after she retired from the library in 2010. Mel said he and Fabian Kite spoke to every person Ursula spoke with for more than a few harsh words. Not one of them was her killer. Everyone had a rock-solid alibi. None of those people had a motive. In Mel's opinion, although two grand doesn't seem like a lot of money, if they were young, desperate for a fix, and high before they reached Shaftesbury Road, then the violence was understandable. Jefferson blamed the lack of a result on Ormrod. He had the girl in his jewellery shop for longer than Dillon. It wasn't the first deal where Ormrod might have got offered stolen goods for quick cash. Ormrod should have been more watchful. Jefferson reckoned he knew the girl and had previously agreed to fence the stuff for her. Jefferson valued the jewellery at six grand and said if we ever find Kite, he will support that figure."

"What do we think, team?" asked Gus.

"There was someone Ursula spoke to that Jefferson never found, guv? Is that what you're thinking?"

"Who could it be, Neil, and where?" said Gus. "If it

were the library, surely Monica Butterworth would have mentioned them. The minister will know his congregation so that that number won't be wildly adrift. Don Hillier confirmed that Ursula wasn't that friendly with Charles Marshall or Beryl Giddings, her nearest neighbours. Who was it that Blessing suggested yesterday? Oh, the postman. They checked him, and his alibi was sound."

"Hang on, guv," said Lydia, "Ursula shouted at someone in the field, didn't she? Perhaps that Hurley character that tried to close the footpath."

"Good thinking. Fewer people would know about that, and he lives outside Mere. He's probably only there for short periods if he has a place in London. Hurley is someone Jefferson could have missed."

"You had a go at me about a lack of walking, guv," said Neil. "Ursula walked into town a minimum of three times a week even after she retired, and that's a fair old distance. How many houses did Ursula pass? There could be dozens of people she met. How did Jefferson arrive at his number of twelve; did they make a public appeal? Did they ask the public to come forward if they argued with Ursula or even pass the time of day when they saw her walking into town? I have little faith in that number, guv."

"There's plenty to keep us busy," said Gus. "Today, we stay on track with the interviews we've got planned. Lydia, I want you to remain in the office. Contact the Hub and get as much data on the good people of Mere between 2010 and 2013 as possible. Highlight the small number of those with a criminal record. Double your efforts on the hunt for Fabian Kite, and then plot the route Ursula took when walking into town using the map on the wallboard. We'll carry out a door-to-door if necessary. We must trace more people Ursula could have antagonised. Luke, when you and

Neil head through Mere on the way to Ringwood, could you do me a favour? Drop these keys back to Arthur Wakeley. Also, chat with his son, Matthew, during his lunch break. He could have played a part in this, even if his alibi held up five years ago. Leave no stone unturned is the order of the day. Right, Blessing, let's go."

Gus found the forty-five-minute journey passed quicker this morning. Blessing was becoming more at ease in his company. Of course, he was still the boss, but as with the other team members, they realised that Gus favoured his colleagues working *with* him rather than *for* him.

"What a beautiful morning," said Blessing as they crossed Salisbury Plain. "The cathedral spire is a wonderful sight in the distance, isn't it?"

"It's the same as everything else, Blessing," said Gus. "When you work in its shadow for forty years, you forget it's there."

"I hope I don't grow to think of it like that," said Blessing.

That's me told, thought Gus. I've become cynical in my old age.

Gus parked the Focus on Castle Street, and he and Blessing walked to the Church on North Street.

Horace Plant met them at the entrance to the mid-Victorian building.

"Welcome," he said, "Your colleague Luke Sherman said you needed my help."

"My name is Freeman, a consultant with Wiltshire Police. My colleague is Detective Constable Umeh. We're taking a fresh look into the death of one of your congregation. I'm sure you remember Ursula Wakeley. She worshipped at your church throughout her life."

"I wasn't alive for much of it. Let's go inside. We have a quiet private room where we can talk about Ursula."

Horace Plant led them to a small room off the entrance hall. There were four hard-backed chairs placed around a small square table. Blessing noticed the lack of decoration throughout the room.

"Ursula could be difficult at times," said the minister. "We understood her; many others in town didn't share her beliefs. It was a terrible shock to hear that she was dead. How anyone could take the life of another human being is a mystery. We did everything in our power to help the police. What is it you think they missed?

"Well, they never found her killer," said Gus. "So, either someone lied to the police and one or more alibis were false, or those who gave statements omitted the name of a possible suspect for the police to investigate. Mere is a tiny town. The killer likely lived among you. Therefore, someone hid relevant facts from the detectives."

"I refuse to believe any of our members could be responsible for such a heinous act. What Gideon and his parents would have made of it, I dread to think. Ursula's father died before I came to this town, but the family reputation for godliness survives."

"Can you give me background on the church Gideon Wakeley's parents and grandparents attended?" asked Gus.

"The Primitive Methodists saw themselves as practising a purer form of Christianity, closer to the earliest Methodists," said Horace Plant. "Their chapels were of simple design and drew their congregation from the poorer members of society. Among the agricultural labourers, they found those who appreciated the themes of damnation, salvation, saints, and sinners. Their direct, spontaneous and passionate style attracted a strong following in these parts."

"They promoted a revival in religious fervour hand-in-hand with social reform," said Gus, "if I remember my schooling correctly."

"Wiltshire was a fertile breeding ground, Mr Freeman. There was unrest in the countryside in the middle of the nineteenth century. The Tolpuddle Martyrs lived just thirty miles away. The Primitive Methodist preachers held large open-air meetings. They presented God as one whose powers could be called upon by preachers. Anecdotal evidence exists of a disabled person getting healed through her conversion to Primitive Methodism."

"I take that with a pinch of salt," said Gus. "Anyway, the original church had long gone when Gideon was born."

"Brother Gideon was born in 1910, Mr Freeman, and baptised in our church. Gideon got married, worshipped here, and now lies at rest in the churchyard. Times have changed. Since the Seventies, many of those different denominations have disappeared under the umbrella of the United Reform Church. Hence the building we now occupy. Attitudes on damnation and salvation have softened. We spread a more modern message now."

"Despite most parishioners following the guidance of their church elders, several continued to hold more extreme beliefs. Is that what you're saying?"

"It's fair to say that Gideon Wakeley and his family opposed the relaxation of our approach to certain human frailties."

"You referred to him as Brother Gideon," said Gus.

"The Primitives used to call one another Brother and Sister. Of course, we don't do that these days, but Gideon's belief was so entrenched in the past that I'm afraid he acquired that nickname. Nobody ever dared say it to his face."

"Did Arthur follow in his father's footsteps?"

"Arthur does not worship here now. I believe he stopped attending soon after his father died. Ursula and her mother, Elspeth, never faltered in their faith. Ursula was at both morning and evening services on Sunday before she died, as she was every week."

"We've spoken to people at the library and various shops in town," said Gus. "Ursula was fond of the occasional biblical phrase. She aimed them at people she thought were less diligent in following the Ten Commandments than was proper."

"Her parents were strict, Mr Freeman, and I won't say her view was misguided. The modern world is a wicked place. Ursula never married, but she had strong views on the behaviour of those that married and then sinned."

"*God will judge the sexually immoral and adulterous,*" said Blessing.

"Your colleague is well-versed in the scriptures, Mr Freeman," said Horace Plant.

"The police are a broad church too these days, Mr Plant," said Blessing. "Diversity is necessary in our armoury when dealing with a wicked world."

"Did Ursula quote the scriptures in this church, Mr Plant?" asked Gus. "Was there anyone, in particular, she attacked for their shortcomings? If there were, then they're people we need to interview. The police might never have tested their alibis for that Wednesday night five years ago."

"Ursula didn't stand in the middle of the church and point the finger at an adulterer, Mr Freeman. Ursula made her comments in passing or as the congregation left the premises. Frequently, the man or woman she accused never heard what she said. It would be wrong of me to suspect someone of murder on that basis."

"I get it. Your church would be empty if you accused everyone you suspected of not living up to Ursula Wakeley's high standards," said Gus.

"You might say that, but I could not possibly comment."

"Thank you for your time, Mr Plant," said Gus, "as always, if we have further questions, we'll get in touch. Please get in touch with us if you hear something that might help our investigations. I don't intend to quit on this case until we find Ursula's killer."

Gus and Blessing left the church and headed for Castle Street.

"You didn't tell me whether I should participate in the interview, guv," said Blessing. "I hope I didn't do wrong by speaking out."

"Not a problem, Blessing," said Gus, "we learn more about each other daily. I should have briefed you on how I wanted the meeting to go. I remember telling Lydia I wanted her to observe and not contribute to one interview we did together early on. Lydia ignored me, and her questions threw the case wide open."

"Andy Carlton used to tell me to start with a plan and then forget it if the witness takes you in an unexpected direction. He said I would soon know if they were leading me away from the truth. If that were the case, I had to get my planned questions back on track."

"Andy and I use the same approach. I let Horace fill in the history of the Wakeley family. Part of it I knew after speaking to Arthur, and I guessed the rest, and Horace didn't disappoint."

"I thought my childhood was strict, but it was heaven compared to what Arthur and Ursula endured. My father has never raised a hand to me."

"Did you placate your mother when she rang last night?"

"It was a close-run thing, guv. I kept my fingers crossed when I mentioned you and Suzie."

"That's hard when you're holding a mobile phone," said Gus, "well done."

"Where do we go next, guv?" asked Blessing.

"Back to the office, why?"

"They do great toasted teacakes in a place on the corner over there."

"Lead on, DC Umeh, but you're paying, as it was your suggestion."

LUKE AND NEIL left Lydia in conversation. She'd finally located Fabian Kite. Lydia gave them a wave as they entered the lift.

"Are we making progress?" asked Luke as they left the lift and walked to the cars.

"I think so," said Neil. "It's hard to tell. Whoever killed Ursula hasn't made catching them easy, that's for sure. Where does Matthew Wakeley work?"

"A wine merchant," said Luke, "we're meeting him near the Old Brewery. Have we got time to drop these keys back first?"

"We do, but I want to hang on to them for another hour. Gus and Lydia looked around the murder site yesterday. It can't harm us to see whether we can find something they missed."

"You're taking a chance, Neil," said Luke, "Gus will blow a fuse if he thinks you're checking his work."

"Leave no stone unturned, Gus said. Something puzzled me from the outset on this one. Why didn't Ursula realise someone had broken in through the kitchen door? Perhaps another person distracted her at the front window, giving the burglar a chance to creep up and whack Ursula over the head. We assumed that Ursula tried to draw the curtains but failed. Why? Not why did she do it, but why did she fail? Her blood was on the carpet close to her fireside chair, so she moved back from the window because of what she saw outside. I want to check the distances and time involved in each step. You'll be the burglar, and I'll be Ursula."

"The mask the man outside was wearing frightened her," said Luke. "The girl broke in, and she was smaller, light on her feet. Ursula didn't hear her."

"We'll see," said Neil. "Who's driving?"

"I'll drive," said Luke.

They saw Matthew Wakeley standing outside the gates of the Old Brewery as they pulled up and parked.

"Fifty-seven, married with grown-up children," said Neil. "He doesn't look like a Wakeley, does he?"

"Matthew must take after his mother, Glenda," said Luke. "He's put weight on in middle age, so there's a warning for you, Neil."

Thirty minutes later, they let Matthew get back to what remained of his lunch hour.

"Well, that was a waste of time," said Neil, "and he never asked us if we wanted to taste the product he sells."

"Look, his alibi is still good, Matthew wasn't involved, but we learned something. Arthur and Glenda often met Ursula in that café you visited yesterday. Perhaps a month before her death, Matthew urgently wanted to speak to his father. So, while in town, he dropped by the café to have a word. Matthew approached their table near the window and looked at Ursula. Even though he was only a yard away, she didn't notice him as she watched Glenda closely. He thought that odd."

"We're back to the question I posed days ago," said Neil, "was Ursula hard of hearing."

Luke drove them across to Shaftesbury Road and parked outside the bungalow.

"It's remote, alright," said Neil, "we'd have to be right out of luck for someone to report seeing strangers."

"The quicker we get inside, the better, just in case," said Luke.

They stood in the hallway and listened. There wasn't even a dripping tap.

"Right," said Neil, "You go to the kitchen door. I'll stand by the fireplace facing the window."

"I've got a flashlight app on my mobile phone," said Luke. "thank goodness."

"Me too," said Neil. "Let me know when you're in position."

"Ready."

Both detectives played out the events from the murder file.

Luke tapped Neil on the shoulder.

"Thirty-two seconds," said Neil. "Do you think she had folded her square of cloth to speed up entry? How many drawers were there in the kitchen?"

"Three," said Luke, "and the panes of glass look solid. The stone from the rockery must have been heavy to break in with less than three blows."

"So, it could be closer to forty seconds. While waiting for you to arrive, I hurried to the window, and half drew the curtains. Then I walked backwards, not taking my eye off the window. If Ursula had turned, she would have seen the burglar."

"How long did you have to wait before I tapped your shoulder?"

"Eight seconds," said Neil, "it felt like a lifetime."

"If the girl took longer to get inside and went to the third kitchen drawer before finding the knife, Ursula stood there, terrified, for up to twenty seconds."

"There was more terror to follow in the bedroom before the killer blow," said Neil. "I'm even more convinced now that Ursula didn't hear her attackers, whether they were inside or out."

"Hang on, look, the television plug is still in the wall socket," said Luke. "We could check the volume setting if we had power."

"My flashlight app's draining my battery. I vote we take the TV to Arthur's house and ask if we can try it out. Any sign of a remote over by that chair?"

"Found it," said Luke. "I wonder whether anyone removed the batteries? They did; okay, we need to put the TV in the car's boot and phone Arthur to say we're coming. We have to drive through town to reach their estate. We can pick up batteries on the way."

Twenty minutes later, Neil rang the front doorbell at Arthur's house. Glenda answered the door.

"DS Neil Davis, Mrs Wakeley, we rang you earlier."

Glenda looked over Neil's shoulder at Luke, carrying a TV.

"You only needed to drop the keys back," she said. "We don't want that old thing."

"We want to try an experiment, Mrs Wakeley," said Luke. "We suspect your sister-in-law was deaf but hid it from you."

"What nonsense," said Glenda. "What will you think of next?"

Luke carried the TV into the kitchen, placed it gently on the marble worktop and plugged it in. He attached the indoor aerial he'd brought from Shaftesbury Road.

Luke fitted two new batteries into the remote control and pressed the 'On' button.

"TURN THAT DOWN!" shouted Arthur Wakeley walking in from the hallway, "What's going on? Who are you?"

"It's the police again, Arthur. I told you less than half an hour ago that they were coming."

"Do you believe us now, Mrs Wakeley?" asked Luke. "Ursula's hearing must have deteriorated. Her colleagues at the library mentioned nothing. Your son Matthew put us on the right track. He said she used to lip-read a month before she died. So, between when she retired and the day of the murder, she heard less and less. The only way she could watch this TV was to have the volume at a painful level. We'll take it with us to show Mr Freeman. Here are your keys. If we need to revisit the bungalow, we'll call you."

Glenda saw them to the door. Arthur returned to the living room without a word.

"I didn't know," said Glenda, "honestly, I had no idea. Why didn't she say?"

"We can't know that, Mrs Wakeley. No doubt Ursula had her reasons."

Luke drove away from the Wakeley house. In his rear-view mirror, he saw Glenda standing by the front door.

"I know what she's thinking," said Luke.

"The silent terror her sister-in-law suffered," said Neil.

"Onwards to Ringwood," said Luke. "We're cutting it fine for our two o'clock. But it was worth it."

IN THE OLD Police Station office, Lydia Logan Barre had completed the tasks Gus had set her. Fabian Kite had reluctantly given her a statement. The Hub promised her figures by the end of play tomorrow. Lydia glanced at the clock. It was past one o'clock. Neil and Luke would be en route to the jewellery shops. Gus and Blessing should be back by now.

Two minutes later, the lift descended to the ground floor. Gus and Blessing had arrived.

"I wondered whether you'd got lost," said Lydia.

"I wasn't driving," said Blessing, "or we would have done."

"How did it go?" asked Lydia.

"I can confirm that the toasted teacakes in Jenny Medcroft's café are excellent," said Gus. "They taste even better when you don't pay for them."

"I've got Fabian Kite's statement, guv," said Lydia, "and we can start work on the Mere census data first thing Friday morning."

"Well done," said Gus, "what did Kite have to say?"

"Ormrod was a dodgy character, guv. Kite believed Ormrod recognised the girl but pleaded ignorance when questioned. Ormrod got done for handling stolen goods a year later. It was a Category Three offence for items between one and ten thousand pounds. He received a one-year sentence. His partner kept the shop open, and Ormrod's back behind the counter now. I mentioned the evaluation without revealing what Jefferson said, and Kite immediately told me the rings alone had to be worth five grand."

"What is Kite doing now?" asked Gus.

"I asked, but he said personal security and volunteered nothing further."

"Luke and Neil will go in cold," said Gus, "which might be no bad thing. Ormrod will be evasive, but Neil and Luke will spot it a mile away. I can't wait to hear what they say when they return."

"Did you learn much from the Methodist minister?" asked Lydia.

"You must wait and see," said Gus. "Blessing and I will update the Freeman Files with our impressions and observations. Horace Plant shared the same opinion of Ursula that people like Monica Butterworth expressed. She spoke up on matters that concerned her but never had a face-to-face showdown with anyone who took great exception to her views."

"Careless whispers can often do more damage, guv," said Blessing.

Not for the first time, Gus congratulated himself on listening to Geoff Mercer's advice.

She might hold polar opposite views to him on religion, but Blessing Umeh could become a valuable addition to the Crime Review Team.

Life is all about balance, after all.

Chapter Ten

LUKE AND NEIL left the A338 Salisbury Road and wormed their way through the busy streets of the market town of Ringwood.

"This is a bigger town than I thought," said Neil. "It's bigger than Devizes."

"Yeah, I guess it's closer to Warminster," said Luke. "We're heading for Southampton Road and the High Street. Where's best to park?"

"There's a car park on Southampton Road, one hundred yards from Ormrod's shop. So we can walk the rest of the way to High Street for Dillon's place. I wonder what that pub is like?"

"The Crown Tap," said Luke, "we don't have time, Neil. Did you see that house further along the road? Did some brickwork look newer to you?"

"You don't miss much, Luke, do you? Maybe someone tried to park in their front room; stranger things have happened. That car park is sixty yards to our right. Time to get on our game head."

Luke and Neil stood outside Ormrod, the jewellers, waiting to gain entry.

"He's upped his security since 2013, then," said Neil.

When Luke heard the buzz, he pushed open the door, and they walked inside. William Ormrod stood behind the counter, watching them.

"How can I help you?"

"Sorry we're ten minutes late, Mr Ormrod," said Luke. "this case has taken a few unexpected turns since we reopened it. When we spoke on the phone to arrange this meeting, I told you that Gus Freeman might visit you, but he asked DS Davis and myself to do the honours."

"You're all coppers. It makes no odds to me. I can't add to what I told the other lot five years back."

"Who did you talk to?" asked Neil.

"His name was Kite, full of himself that one. He thought I had something to do with it somehow."

"In what way, Mr Ormrod? You didn't know the victim, did you?"

"Of course not. I've never been to Mere. Kite reckoned I knew the girl that brought me the jewellery, and she'd offered me stuff before. That was rubbish."

"Are you saying you recognised the girl?"

"I'd never spoken to her, yet she looked familiar. Her scarf and hair hid most of her face. The quality of her clothes set her apart from most people who come here. We cater to the masses. The value of the items on display amounts to a tidy sum, but you won't find rings and necklaces here where the price tag makes your eyes water. I reckon that girl and her family frequent a much more refined establishment."

"I spoke to a colleague of ex-DI Kite yesterday," said Luke, "he suggested the items were worth far more than your original estimate. You offered to take the goods off the young lady's hands for a mere two hundred and fifty pounds. You must have licked your lips at what a profit you would make."

"What if I did? She wasn't interested in the money. I could have told her the lot was worth barely twenty quid, and she would have still taken the money and left in a hurry. Instead, all she wanted to do was get shot of it."

"You knew they were hot," said Neil. "Why didn't you ring the police?"

"You're a comedian. My margins are small on the quality of the product I offer. You make it up on deals where the punter doesn't know what they've got. It's not personal; it's just business."

"Did you ever see the girl again?" asked Neil.

"Hardly," replied Ormrod with a smile.

"What about the guy she was with," asked Luke, "was he from the same part of town as the girl?"

"I couldn't tell from here. I don't stand by the door to check where a customer goes next. So I moved on to something else once she was outside the door."

"Did you have customers waiting?" asked Luke.

"No, I'd just got rid of two couples searching for engagement rings. The place was empty when the girl walked through the door. She was in and out in two minutes. Kite asked me that back then. He wanted to know whether anyone else could identify the girl. Before you ask, I put back the trays of rings I'd shown the ones that came in before her."

Luke glanced over at Neil, and a quick nod confirmed his thoughts. They wouldn't learn much more. Nevertheless, Luke was happy that they'd found a helpful lead.

"We'll let you get on with your day, Mr Ormrod," said Luke.

"Mind how you go," said Ormrod as they left the store.

"I've not spent much time in jewellery stores," said Neil. "Good customer service wasn't high on his priorities, was it?"

"I reckon Ormrod is a rogue on the quiet," said Luke. "I wonder whether Bartholomew Dillon got made from the same cloth?"

"If the name's anything to go by, he's different class," said Neil.

As they entered Dillon's, the tinkle of the bell reminded Luke of an art gallery in Bath he'd recently visited. The shop looked quaint rather than functional, and its owner emerged from a back room. Bartholomew Dillon was seventy if he was a day, his round face topped with tufts of white hair. He wore a red cardigan over a white shirt with a button-down collar. His glasses hung around his neck on a gold chain.

"Good afternoon," he said, "you must be the policemen I was expecting. You're early."

"We completed our business with one of your colleagues quicker than we thought," said Luke.

"Ah, you've been to Ormrod's. I don't class him as a colleague. My father started this shop a century ago, and we've always strived to maintain a reputation for honesty."

"We did wonder," said Neil.

"Ormrod served time for handling stolen goods," said Dillon. "I'm surprised you didn't know."

Neil wondered how that slipped through the net, but it explained why Ormrod smiled when asked if he'd seen the girl again after that day.

"I need not tell you why we're here, Mr Dillon," said

Luke. "My colleague and I are taking another crack at the Ursula Wakeley murder case. The sale of her jewellery was one instance where the original investigation hoped to unearth suspects. If they identified the two people who had the jewellery so soon after the murder, it might have led to an early arrest."

"Five years is a long time," said Dillon, "I barely remember what happened now."

"You suspected you were getting offered stolen goods by the young lady straight away, is that right?" asked Neil.

"You get a sixth sense," said Dillon. "She was furtive, in a hurry to make a deal. It didn't feel genuine. I didn't dare take the risk. She left at once."

"Can you recall anything that stood out?" asked Neil.

"It was so long ago,"

"Let's do this another way," said Luke. "Take a seat. Close your eyes. Think about those few minutes she was in your shop. Then, I'll fire questions at you and want you to say the first thing that comes into your head."

"If you're sure," said Bartholomew Dillon, sitting on a chair by the counter.

"Age?"

"Sixteen to eighteen."

"Tall or short?"

"Tall."

"Hair colour?"

"Brunette. Long hair, but stylishly cut."

"Winter coat?"

"Full length, designer label, or an excellent copy."

"Voice?"

"Educated."

"Gloves?"

"Yes, but…"

"Something else?"

"When she stretched out her hand to collect the jewellery, I saw a watch. It looked to be an Omega Seamaster. Again, it might have been a copy."

"The young man who waited outside the shop. Tall or short?"

"I never saw anyone."

"Okay," said Luke, "that's better. Thank you, Mr Dillon. Just one more thing. Did the girl look familiar?"

"I couldn't say," said Dillon. "I get people of all ages through my door. I might have seen her before, but placing the sighting in context is difficult. If she walked through the door now, I might recognise her, but I couldn't swear to it with a different hairstyle, summer clothes, high heels instead of boots."

"So you never saw her again?" asked Neil.

"Definitely not," said Bartholomew Dillon, "people can come to Ringwood from a wide area, Detective. Your colleagues believed she came from Mere. But she might not have lived in that small town or the Ringwood area. Thirty miles is no distance by car these days. You asked me how old I thought she was. I said between sixteen and eighteen. I don't believe she was older than that, so I'm not surprised I haven't seen her in the past five years. She was an educated young lady, of that I'm certain. So college, university, a gap year, and full-time employment would inevitably follow. I wouldn't expect to see her in the area ever again unless her parents came from around here. That's the way of the world these days, isn't it? I left school at sixteen and started here to learn the trade from my father. I've lived nowhere else but in Ringwood. Times have changed, Detectives. Times have changed."

"Indeed, Mr Dillon," said Luke. "You've been most helpful. Thank you for your time."

Neil and Luke left the shop with a reassuring jingle of the doorbell.

"We keep finding little clues, don't we?" said Neil, rubbing his hands.

"I didn't think we'd learn much from Ormrod, but when he mentioned the girl seemed classy, I realised that helped explain the quality piece of cloth they used to protect themselves from glass shards."

"Good thinking on two occasions," said Neil. "Dillon was drifting with the 'couldn't be sure, it was a long time ago' scenario. Sitting him down and firing questions at him made him remember far more detail. One of those Omega watches has to cost two grand, doesn't it?"

"Who are we looking for, then?" asked Luke. "A rich girl that got mixed up with a local hooligan; or two kids from well-to-do families? We need to get this information back to Gus."

"We might be on the right track at last," said Neil.

"Dillon was right, of course," said Luke. "You and I showed today that a car could sit outside Ursula's bungalow without raising suspicion. That was even easier in the dead of winter on one of the coldest nights of the year. The Hub will give us data, allowing us to isolate names fitting our profile for the killer and his accomplice. They could have come from anywhere if they drove to Shaftesbury Road."

"Wherever they came from, they had met Ursula before that night. It wasn't random."

"Did they meet at the library? Who drives miles to visit Mere library if they had one on their doorstep?"

"A boyfriend might drive to meet a girl," said Neil.

"That's a possibility. We might still find the girl on the 2011 Census. Her partner may come from further afield. So, she was the one with the library card, and he got signed in as a visitor."

"I wonder whether Monica Butterworth has a record of that?" asked Neil.

"Back to the office, and then we'll see what Gus makes of what we've learned."

WHEN THE LADS emerged from the lift, Lydia placed the last pin in the map marking Ursula's walk into town. Gus looked up from his computer.

"Blessing's in the restroom wrestling with the Gaggia," he said. "You might need to rescue her, Neil; she's been a while. So get a coffee, and we'll run through where we've got to today."

When everyone finished their refreshments, Gus listened to Luke and Neil's report.

"Right, get everything updated on the files, and then you can read through what Blessing and I learned from our visit to the Methodist Church. Where's Ursula's TV?"

"Still in the boot of my car, guv," said Luke. "We took it to Arthur Wakeley's testing my theory, but I didn't forward think. Glenda was adamant she didn't want it, so I got stuck with it."

"Store it in the restroom. When we return the murder file and the results of our review to Salisbury nick, the TV can get included to support our conclusions. With luck, we'll have names to give them too. After that, it's down to Salisbury to get the people charged and before a court."

"OK, guv," said Luke. "I'll bring it up later. What we learned altered our opinions about who was responsible and why?"

"I'm happy to discount the robbery element now," said Gus. "The revenge motive is still in the mix. The young couple trying to sell the jewellery could be the same kids tormenting Ursula by canoodling outside the café. They might also be the same two that had a stand-up row with her at the library. Identifying those two is a priority."

"What's the plan for tomorrow, guv?" asked Neil.

"The weather forecast is favourable, Neil. You can see Lydia's handiwork on the street map. The four of you will carry out door-to-door enquiries. I know it's a drag, but we must check Ursula didn't needle someone on her way into town so that they lashed out. We don't get data from the Hub until late tomorrow, so we'd be twiddling our thumbs. Is everyone happy?"

"Ecstatic, guv," said Neil.

"It's not all glamour and teacakes, you know," said Gus, winking at Blessing Umeh.

"Can I recap something, guv?" asked Luke.

"Certainly, Luke. What's on your mind?"

"We never found similar crimes in the region either side of Ursula Wakeley's in 2013; therefore, you dismissed the thrill-seekers theory Blessing suggested. Why not spread the net wider? We have a better profile for our killer now and of our victim. Perhaps the Hub can suggest similar cases elsewhere in the country?"

"Both jewellery shop owners mentioned the girl was well-spoken and dressed in stylish clothes," said Lydia. "Dillon said he'd not expect to see her in Ringwood once she left the area for university or work. What if the killer was a well-educated young man? He could be anywhere in the country after 2013. If he spent three years at university, or more, it would switch his killing fields."

"A tad dramatic, Lydia," said Gus, "but I can't deny I've

not considered Blessing's idea. We need to home in on this boy and girl, find out how they connected to Ursula, and then where they went after the murder. Put in a request for an urgent search routine with the Hub, Lydia. It wouldn't hurt to remind them it's vital we get that 2011 Census material tomorrow as well."

"Will do, guv," said Lydia.

"Can I ask Monica Butterworth whether she has visitor records before 2013, guv," said Neil. "If the young girl is local, she could have signed in a boyfriend. We might get lucky and find two names."

"Call Mrs Butterworth and check, Neil. Under General Data Protection Regulations, certain data is time-limited."

Neil made the call. Monica wasn't working this afternoon, but an assistant confirmed that contact details for library cardholders and visitors were recorded and held for up to seven years. In addition, they kept information regarding PC use, including browsing history, for twelve months. That was to follow the Regulation of Investigation Powers Act 2000.

"We must get a wiggle on," said Gus. "Did she say when they deleted these records?"

"At the end of each calendar month, guv. That means the library should still hold details from July 2011 onwards."

"Right, Neil. That's eighteen months before the murder. The jewellers both put the girl at sixteen to eighteen years old. That narrows our number of potential suspects. The Census covers the Community Area, which will prove useful. It increases the total number of residents from three to four and a half thousand."

"So, we might get her even though she didn't live in Mere itself," said Luke.

"Drive over to the library straight away, Neil. Get a copy

of everything available. We've lost the browsing history, but that's tough luck. No matter how fast we found the connection, we would never have had that."

"OK, guv, I'll see everyone in the morning. Evening all."

Neil disappeared to the lift.

"Jefferson and Kite could have followed up on that information, guv," said Lydia. "If they hadn't focussed their attention on the robbery."

"Spilt milk, Lydia," said Gus. "It's half-past four now. Why don't we finish for the day? Luke, are you taking Blessing home tonight?"

Luke nodded.

"I'll wait for Alex to get here from London Road, guv," said Lydia. "It's his physio again this evening, and then we'll grab a bite to eat together before I head home."

"I aim to get to my allotment before six," said Gus. "An hour's work on the land will allow me time to think through everything we've learned. It feels like we're on the homeward leg now. By the time we wrap things up for the week on Friday afternoon, I hope to have two names to pass to our colleagues at Salisbury."

Gus left the others to finish up and headed for the lift. If he was quick, he could miss the worst of the traffic. He sailed through Seend and breezed along London Road. Someone up there was looking after him. Blessing Umeh must have put in a word on his behalf.

After a change of clothes, Gus left the car at the bungalow and walked to the allotment. Bert Penman and Clemency Bentham were hard at work. Gus acknowledged them and opened the shed. Five minutes later, he identified four things he could tackle that allowed him to switch off and collect his thoughts on the case.

Gus was drawing the soil up around the base of his Brussel sprouts to stimulate extra root growth while considering the telecentre Neil described. What could explain the interest Ursula Wakeley appeared to show? Witnesses said Ursula loved to read. What did she read? Monica Butterworth implied it was primarily English literature, not books on how to hack into the Pentagon.

Every teenager Ursula came across in the library would have used smartphones to access their social media accounts. But unfortunately, Ursula only had a landline at the bungalow and no mobile, tablet, or laptop. So, anything Ursula did got carried out inside the four walls of the telecentre. If she had any browsing history, then it was long gone.

"Hi, Gus. I hope I'm not disturbing you?"

It was Brett Penman.

"Hello, Brett," said Gus, "good to see you. I suppose you've come to collect Bert. He and Clemency generally finish gardening by seven at the latest. Your grandfather likes to check the Lamb is still keeping his cider properly. How's the job hunt going?"

"I've made a start, Gus, and secured an interview at the end of next week for a position in Wootton Bassett. I'm still waiting on replies from three others. I arranged to meet my grandfather and Clemency tonight. We're dining together at the Lamb."

"You don't hang around, do you?"

"I don't know what you mean," laughed Brett. "Is Suzie around later?"

"Suzie is working in Swindon at present. We don't have firm plans for tonight, but it's Wednesday, so it wouldn't surprise me if she dropped by the bungalow on her way home. Will you be dashing off as soon as you've eaten? If not, then maybe I can persuade her to come for a late drink."

"You know my grandfather. Unless they bring in a curfew, he'll be in the Lamb until its regular closing time. Maybe we'll see you later."

Brett walked over to join Bert. Clemency pretended to continue hoeing, but she cleared the weeds from the same piece of ground several times before Brett gave her a wave. Finally, the church clock struck seven, and his three friends made their way towards the gateway.

Ten minutes later, Gus realised he couldn't get his head back into the telecentre mystery without food and drink. It was ages since he'd had that toasted teacake. He cleaned his tools, replaced them in the shed, and after checking the lock, he made his way along the lane to the bungalow.

Suzie's GTI was in the driveway. The living room window was open, and sounds of Fleetwood Mac drifted over the lawn. Gus walked into the hallway and recognised a familiar smell from the kitchen.

"Sweet and sour chicken," he sighed, "perfect."

The chef appeared in the doorway.

"Did you have a good day?"

"We made progress," said Gus,

"Me too," said Suzie, "but that was because Gareth was off today."

"Brett's treating Bert and Clemency to a meal at the Lamb tonight," said Gus. "We'll be welcome for a drink if we wander along later. What do you say?"

"It sounds like a plan," said Suzie. "Why are you dubious about your progress?"

Gus explained over dinner, which they ate in the living room accompanied by Fleetwood Mac.

"Very Agatha Christie," said Suzie, "but with computers instead of poison pen letters."

"Which one was that?" asked Gus.

"The Moving Finger," said Suzie. "A brother and sister arrived in a small village and soon received an anonymous letter accusing them of being lovers, not siblings. More letters get delivered to other villagers. Someone of importance is found dead, and a letter lay beside her body."

"Were the accusations false," asked Gus, "or did any have the ring of truth?"

"They were false. The police concluded the letter writer was a middle-aged woman, but Miss Marple proved it was the first victim's husband. The letters were a diversion. Do you have an adulterer in the town whose lover has two of his children running around?"

"Not as far as we know," said Gus, "Ursula Wakeley accused someone of adultery in church after a Sunday morning service. It seems too far-fetched to me. We have zero evidence Ursula was computer literate. The anecdotal evidence suggests she had a wicked tongue and whispered her accusations behind people's backs."

"She sounds an unpleasant woman," said Suzie, "but as you say, it's a stretch to imagine she could wage an online smear campaign against people she disliked."

"That gives me an idea," said Gus. "I'll get Blessing to search for Ursula online."

"Are you serious? If Ursula sent disparaging comments to people, she wouldn't log on under her name. None of the town's teenagers would accept a Friend Request from a seventy-eight-year-old woman with her reputation. They would block her after the first time she tried to contact them. On the other hand, if she spent a fair bit of time in that computer room and nobody came forward to complain, she was doing something normal like researching her family tree."

"If Ursula attacked people who attended the library, surely they confronted her, either while she still worked there or on one of her many visits after she retired. I don't know enough about these different sites. I'll let Blessing look. We've got nothing to lose."

"I hope you're not going to the pub in your gardening clothes," said Suzie. "I had a shower and changed as soon as I arrived here. Time for you to get moving."

"Yes, boss," said Gus.

They found Brett, Bert, and Clemency sitting inside the bar.

"Not used to the heat, Brett?" asked Suzie.

"You wait until the winter," he scolded, "you Brits complain at a dusting of snow. We keep going regardless of how much the skies throw at us."

"Who's ready for a drink?" asked Gus.

"You timed your arrival to perfection," said Bert, emptying his glass.

Nothing changes thought Gus. Thank goodness.

Thursday, 5 July 2018

GUS WAS up with the lark. Suzie was still asleep. His assumption that Bert Penman wouldn't leave the Lamb until last orders was correct. When Gus and Suzie walked along the lane to the bungalow, Bert ambled beside them. Brett and Clemency were five yards ahead.

"Is Brett seeing the Reverend home, Bert?" asked Gus.

"Her bicycle is outside my house," said Bert. "The

Reverend came calling for me this afternoon. She's only just started doing that. Brett was out all day. I suppose she thought I could do with the company."

"Brett told me he'd got a job interview next week," said Gus.

"It would be good to see him settled," said Bert.

"You never know," said Suzie.

As they turned into the driveway, Gus heard the Reverend's bell ring twice on her bicycle as she made her way home.

Gus showered and dressed for work. As he stood in the kitchen deciding on breakfast, Suzie emerged from the bedroom.

"No fry-up for me this morning," she said, "something healthy."

"Your wish is my command," said Gus, putting the bacon back in the fridge.

"Apart from getting Blessing to scour the internet, what else is on the list for today?" asked Suzie.

"Nothing for me," said Gus. "I've got the team on a door-to-door, hoping to find the killer will admit everything as soon as they tackle them on their doorstep."

"What was behind that idea?"

"Ursula walked into town several times a week for decades. We wondered whether it was someone she had a running battle with for ages. After years of provocation, that person snapped."

"That sounds like the last throw of the dice, Gus. Last night you said you thought you were nearly there."

"We are if we turn up the names of two posh kids with a penchant for playing noughts and crosses with a knife."

Gus smacked the kitchen table with the palm of his hand. Suzie jumped.

"That's not something we've investigated. We thought the girl might have left the bungalow with the jewellery, leaving the killer behind alone with his victim. We knew the approximate time of death. He could have tormented Ursula before stabbing her in the heart. The autopsy report said the killer continued to experiment with the body and that *they* played a game of noughts and crosses."

"You didn't realise the ambiguity in that statement?" said Suzie.

"I'm not making excuses, but the ACC and Geoff Mercer read the murder report before handing it over to me. They noticed nothing amiss. Jefferson and Kite wrapped up the investigation and put it into storage five years ago with no reference to both intruders staying with the body until the bitter end. The guy who did the autopsy may not even be around now to check. That will be my first job when I reach the office. First, I have to confirm whether anyone thought two different people did the cuts on the right arm. Or am I guilty of second-guessing every statement I read because I'm not as sharp as I once was? Why didn't that hit me in the face as soon as I read it the first time?"

"Don't beat yourself up. The coroner should have known better than to sign off on a report that left doubt. Imagine if the case had gone to court. Both defence counsels would have argued the other party was responsible for everything. The prosecution could never prove who did it beyond a reasonable doubt. Jefferson and his team dodged a bullet. If you can clarify that statement and find the killers, then Salisbury can finally get justice for Ursula Wakeley."

"I love you," said Gus. "I thought I was heading for a quiet day in the office, waiting for my team to return from pounding the streets. A conversation over the breakfast table throws up a clue that could be gold dust."

"I love you too," said Suzie, "although I'm not sure why it's so valuable."

"Blessing Umeh suggested these two were thrill-seekers."

"Killers who derive immense satisfaction from the process of murder," said Suzie. "The act of tracking their victim, rather than the killing itself. They crave the euphoric adrenaline rush provided by stalking and capturing their victim. These two went further, though, didn't they? They enjoyed the post-mortem experience every bit as much. They must have killed again."

"Five years have passed," said Gus. "How many bodies are there out there?"

"And where do you start to look?"

"First, we find the two intruders, even if it means trekking to the summit of Machu Picchu. Then we seek help from the local police to identify potential victims."

"I bet you never expected to get handed a case like this when they tempted you out of retirement."

Gus took Suzie in his arms. Suddenly, he felt exhausted.

"I never expected a lot of things," he said.

"Any regrets?"

"Not one."

Chapter Eleven

WHEN HE ARRIVED at the Old Police Station office, Gus found the rest of the team preparing for their version of the Long March. He sensed they weren't looking forward to it, but it was time they learned how hard it was to be an officer on the beat. He'd had enough experience of it when he pounded the streets of Salisbury forty years ago.

"You've got a good day for it," he said. "Have you decided on your pairings?"

"I'm with Blessing," said Neil.

"We'll play it by ear, guv," said Luke. "If the home-owner responds better to Lydia, I'll take a back seat and vice versa."

"That works for me," said Gus. "Who decides which questions you ask? Or were you going to wing it?"

"What do you recommend, guv," asked Lydia.

"Be polite, convince them they're doing you a huge favour, and speak to as many of them as possible before getting back here by half-past four."

"Do we leave a note at places where we get no reply?" asked Blessing.

"Look, the chances are you won't find someone who coughs to the murder within two minutes of opening the door. You'll return with nothing except further confirmation that Ursula was difficult to love. But, whatever you do, don't get bored and let your concentration drift. I guarantee somebody will give you information we've not heard before. Please ensure you get that snippet of information and bring it back this afternoon. Got it?"

"Yes, guv," came the group response. They started to move towards the lift.

"Hold on," said Gus. "In case you wonder whether I'll be sat here with my feet up all day, I thought of something last night. When we got the murder file, the autopsy report intimated that the two intruders moved her into the bedroom after Ursula got struck with that horse statue. The timing wasn't exact, but we assumed it was around ten o'clock."

"I remember we stepped through the sequence of events, guv. There was no way we could tell when the drawers of the dressing table got rifled," said Neil. "We wondered whether the girl left with the jewellery and wasn't involved in the murder."

"Neil argued that because they didn't bring a weapon, the girl grabbed a kitchen knife to scare Ursula and hadn't planned to murder her," said Luke.

"It's hard to imagine a woman taking part in what followed after Ursula moved to the bedroom," said Blessing. "We concluded the female left because it made sense if robbery was the reason for the break-in."

"What if it wasn't?" asked Lydia. "What if they worked

together from start to finish? It doesn't bear thinking about."

"Suzie and I discussed the case last night. When I mentioned what you were doing today, she thought the door-to-door was the action of a desperate man. I replied without thinking that everything would be fine if we turned up the names of two posh kids with a penchant for playing noughts and crosses with a knife."

"Well, it would," said Neil. "So, what did that start you thinking?"

"Because the wording in the autopsy report suggested that the killer enjoyed playing with the body after death. The stab to the heart took place in the bedroom between ten and midnight. The cuts and slashes to Ursula's torso could have occurred within minutes or over the next few hours. The report said, 'they played noughts and crosses' on the right arm."

"Oh, that's gross," said Lydia. "It was bad enough thinking a young man did that to her, but for both to stand over Ursula's naked body handing the knife to one another and taking their turn in a children's game is grotesque."

"Blessing appears to have had the right idea," said Gus. "This murder was planned and executed by two people who enjoyed the experience. No way will this be the only time they acted together. I'll confirm with the coroner that different hands did the cuts and then spread the net across the country for further examples of their handiwork. If these two left to go on to college or university, my guess is they stayed close and continued to kill. They're sick, and we must stop their spree."

The room fell silent.

"What are you waiting for?" asked Gus, "get out there and find someone who remembers Ursula crossing swords with two students or teenagers. I want those names. Forget the people we've already spoken to for now. I'll run through the digital files to see whether there was anything in their statements we missed. Something we can use to narrow the search."

"We need that data from the Hub, guv," said Lydia. "We might get two hundred names, but it won't take long to filter out those that don't fit the new profile."

Luke, Lydia, Neil, and Blessing headed for the lift. Gus got straight on the phone.

"Geoff Mercer speaking,"

"Geoff, it's Gus. What was the name of the coroner who did the autopsy on Ursula Wakeley? The bloke I dealt with for years in Salisbury was Jimmy Calvert, but he was off sick for a few weeks over Christmas and into the New Year if I remember. Jimmy had a heavy dose of the flu that laid people low that winter."

"They filled in with locums, I think. Let me check. Peter Morgan popped over to Salisbury for two weeks to cover Jimmy around that time. Did you look at the signature at the bottom?"

"I concentrated on the wording in the report," said Gus, "and now I'm wondering whether I misinterpreted the comments. I'm just checking my copy of the murder file, and the signature isn't clear. The bottom inch or two of print on the paper is faint."

"Peter was there, Gus. Sorry, mate, you'll have to give him a ring and hope he doesn't tell you to take a hike."

"Has he found another job yet?" asked Gus.

"He's doing part-time work in Bath and North East Somerset," said Geoff. "I've got a new contact number for him somewhere."

Geoff found the number and passed it on. Gus updated

Geoff on the current state of the case and then called Peter Morgan.

"Peter, it's Gus Freeman. I need your help."

"Oh, you must be kidding?"

"Lives are at stake, Peter. Don't be a prat. When you went to Salisbury at New Year in 2013, you performed an autopsy on a seventy-eight-year-old spinster called Ursula Wakeley. A vicious stabbing and mutilation in Mere. Do you remember it?"

"I'm not likely to forget it," said Morgan. "That bedroom was a set from a horror movie."

"I don't know what Mel Jefferson said to you, but he and Fabian Kite followed the robbery angle because of the missing jewellery. We now believe it was a planned killing from start to finish. Your report stated that the post-mortem cutting looked like the killer was having fun. What did you make of the cuts to the right arm?"

"I think I know what you're asking, Freeman, and I'm afraid I couldn't be certain. As the cuts and slashes progressed down the body, they did become more confident and assured. The game of noughts and crosses was the work of a twisted mind, or minds. Everything could have been a shared act if two people were in that bedroom with the victim after midnight. The only common thing was the blade. The assailant, or assailants, wore gloves and washed and wiped the knife before returning it to the kitchen drawer. It took me two hours to eliminate the other blades in that drawer, Freeman. The murder weapon had been buried deep."

That put a different slant on things. Gus thought the girl had only taken part in the game.

"Why didn't you mention this in the report?" asked Gus.

"I would have been guessing," said Morgan. "It's the

same as determining which hand the killer used. My first thoughts were that the killer was right-handed. However, if you can now confirm two people were in the room for the duration, then if pressed, I think the second person was left-handed. That would explain the nature of the wounds showing a dominant hand throughout."

"If a killer switched from right to left, you expect to be able to tell, is that what you're saying?"

"I've been doing this job for a long time, Freeman. I've carried out hundreds of autopsies. Mel Jefferson chose to concentrate on the jewellery theft, and my thought processes on who did what to whom and when were never going to be of interest. So, I didn't pursue them. I wasn't sure of the chain of events, so I decided it was best to report the facts I had solid evidence to support. Yes, I expect to see the difference between someone switching from their dominant hand. Several things change, depth and angle of cut, hesitation. None of that was present."

"Does that suggest Ursula Wakeley wasn't their first victim?" asked Gus.

"Ah, now that's a tough one, Freeman. We didn't have suspects in custody. They could have been frequent drug users with none of the inhibitions of a first-timer. The differences in the wounds would be marginal. Again, I would be guessing."

"Thank you, Peter. You've been most helpful."

"Class is permanent, Freeman. If you recognise it."

Gus ended the call. Life was too short to argue with Peter Morgan.

Gus contacted London Road again and asked to get through to the Hub.

"I need to speak with DS Alex Hardy. Is he available, please?"

Gus heard the phone get placed on the desk. Thirty seconds can feel like a lifetime when you're in a rush.

"Yes, guv, Alex here. What can I do for you?"

Gus told Alex to use the Hub facility to search for details of unsolved murders of older women, who lived alone, perhaps in remote locations, since 2013.

"Method, guv?"

"Our victim died from a single stab wound, Alex," said Gus. "but you're looking for killers that enjoy stalking their prey. That's a vital part of the experience. They tormented our victim for up to two hours before she died. Then they slashed and mutilated her naked body."

"Was she raped?"

"There was no sexual element whatsoever, Alex," said Gus.

"Leave it with me, guv. I'll drop by the office before the close of play tomorrow. I can update you on the progress I've made. I need to come there because I'm collecting Lydia. We're spending the weekend searching for her father."

"Fair enough. I look forward to seeing you tomorrow. Oh, one more thing. If you uncover similar cases, note any health issues for the victims relating to their sight or hearing."

"Will do, guv," said Alex.

Gus opened his copy of the Freeman Files. Time to review every conversation recorded in the murder file and the interviews they'd held this week.

Four weary travellers returned to the Old Police Station office at a quarter past four.

"Finished so soon?" asked Gus.

"We visited every conceivable house along the route, guv," said Neil. "We ignored non-residential properties such as the Walnut Tree pub. Was Ursula teetotal? Would she stand outside with a placard decrying the demon drink?"

"I think we might have heard before, Neil," Gus said.

"At least a third of them were at work, guv," said Luke. "Or they ignored the bell because they realised who we were."

"Forget the bad stuff, Luke. When do we get to the valuable snippets?"

"Neil and I spoke with a lady who visited the library often," said Blessing. "She's got a mobility scooter these days and only goes to the library once a week. She told us Ursula rowed with two teenagers, maybe eighteen months before the murder. This Mrs Atkins was after a new release by a thriller writer, and she overheard the argument."

"Was this in the library or the telecentre?" asked Gus.

"Library, guv. Ursula Wakeley told the kids they were sitting too close to one another and making too much noise."

"What was their reaction?"

"The girl laughed in her face. The boy stood and towered over Ursula. He accused her of being jealous, not of the girl but of him."

"How did Ursula respond to that?"

"She brandished her steel ruler, guv, and told them if they didn't behave, she would have them thrown out."

"Did Mrs Atkins recognise either of the youngsters?" asked Gus.

"She didn't know their names, but they were only in the library during school holidays, according to her."

"Boarders," said Gus, "at a school charging ten grand a term, I bet. That ties in with our posh kids' theory. Again we're narrowing the field. When we get the Hub data, we'll soon see who she meant."

"Luke and I found someone to corroborate the incident outside the café, guv."

"The kissing couple. Jenny Medcroft's daughter, Mrs Burden, thought they were students, didn't she? Did she mention when that was?"

"It was a year later than the library incident, guv," said Neil.

"How old did Mrs Atkins think those two were," asked Luke.

"Fourteen or fifteen," said Blessing.

"Our kissing students could have been sixteen or seventeen," said Gus. "I wonder if they were one and the same."

"Two and the same, guv," said Neil. "I'll pop in and see if Becky Burden can give a description. We can run that by Mrs Atkins tomorrow."

"The Hub data just appeared in my inbox, guv," said Lydia.

"Don't keep us in suspense, Lydia," said Gus.

"There were two hundred and sixty-four people aged between fifteen and nineteen in the 2011 Census."

"Is that a lot?" asked Blessing.

"Don't worry. We'll soon reduce that first thing in the morning," said Gus. "Start with those in full-time education aged fourteen or fifteen in the summer of 2011. We'll try to identify Mrs Atkins's library trouble makers. If we get names and photos, we can put them in front of the café staff."

"There has to be more, guv," said Lydia. "A skirmish in the library and poking fun at Ursula outside the café a year later wouldn't provoke such a violent reaction, surely?"

"We're not dealing with normal teenagers, Lydia," said Blessing.

"For everyone's sakes, I hope you're right, Blessing," said

Gus. "It's time to call it a day, folks. But, Lydia, ensure each of us has a copy of that file before you leave. Then, first thing in the morning, we start our search."

Friday, 6 July 2018

WHEN GUS PARKED the Focus at the rear of the Old Police Station, he smiled to himself. His team didn't need any encouragement from him. They were already upstairs, and it was only five to nine. Gus had hoped to make it in from Devizes earlier, but the Highways Department must have forgotten something when they completed the road-works in Seend. They were back this morning, digging up tarmac that had hardly had time to settle.

"Morning, everyone," he said as he exited the lift, "what do we know?"

"It's not as straightforward as we hoped, guv," said Lydia.

"At least we've worked out why that is," added Luke.

"The census took place on the twenty-seventh of March, guv," said Lydia, "which was in term time. We checked each of the children recorded in the Mere district aged around fourteen or fifteen, and nobody fitted our profile."

"They were at boarding school," said Gus, "as we suspected. Didn't I read that the 2011 Census attempted to collect more data than in the past? However, they used terms such as 'out of term population' and 'usually resident'. I imagine this has posed problems over the years. For instance, if you took Bath, they have a large student population for a sizeable part of the year. To understand the level of services they need to provide, the County Council needs to know the numbers. For part of the year, the students return home, so their local authority needs access to that data. Overseas students swell the numbers in cities like Bath before flying home in the summer. Did the Hub restrict the search to those counted as 'usually resident' in the Mere district?"

"It did, guv," said Luke, "but supplementary data's available, taking account of the categories you mentioned. I've analysed that and can't find anyone that fits the profile. We're stumped."

"Explain that to me, Neil," asked Gus.

"Students and schoolchildren were initially counted in the usually resident base of their boarding school or university, guv. Then they got relocated to their family home. The family home for our suspects may not be in the Mere district. It could be in Scotland or Northern Ireland. It could conceivably be abroad."

"So, unless we know which schools these two attended back in 2011, we can't find them, guv," said Lydia.

"What about our kids in the library?"

"They wouldn't have been in school uniform, guv," said Luke. "not when Mrs Atkins says she saw them."

"The kissing students?"

"A Saturday afternoon, guv," said Neil, "and they were sixteen or seventeen by then. Many sixth-forms dispense with uniforms from Year 12. You wouldn't know where they studied if it were out of term time."

"The scarf," said Gus, "what about the scarf? Was it recorded? If not, get hold of Ormrod and Dillon, and check whether it was a school or college scarf."

It was a frustrating start to the day as Neil and Luke

called the shop owners while Lydia and Blessing got their heads together. Gus wondered what they were debating.

"Have you had a brainwave, Lydia?" he asked.

"Blessing has, guv."

"Time to share, Blessing."

"Although these students might have been away from Mere for weeks on end, they could still keep in touch with things."

"Letters or phone calls to their parents, asking them to send money and cake. We've seen public school life depicted on TV and film."

"No guv, social media will be their main source of contact to the community."

"We've discussed this before, Blessing. These two kids and anyone Ursula Wakeley argued with would never befriend her on social media. There was no way she could torment them online, and we have no evidence of her ever accessing one of those sites."

"Well, we can't say she didn't, guv," said Blessing, "because the library only retained browsing data for twelve months. What we agreed was Ursula didn't access the internet under her name. Let me dig into the accounts connected to Mere and see what I can find."

"Have you done this before, Blessing?" asked Gus.

"I've used most sites since I was sixteen, guv. My parents barred me from having a mobile phone until then. So when I started working with Andy Carlton, we had a case that needed someone to trawl through posts and messages on Facebook searching for hate speech. He thought I knew my way around better than the middle-aged detectives on his team. I have a knack for it, guv."

"Get started then," said Gus, "we need all the help we can get."

"Ormrod thinks the scarf was woollen and brown to match the winter coat she wore, guv," said Neil.

"Dillon said much the same, guv," said Luke. "It was a long scarf, like Doctor Who wore, but plain. He couldn't remember the colour, but it was dark."

"OK, we're not going to find them via that route. While Blessing and Lydia join forces on the internet, we three could try another approach."

"What about the Electoral Roll, guv," said Neil.

"You need a name to start the search, Neil," said Luke.

"I remember my Dad telling me that back in the old days, he could go to the local church. And on the porch, there was a booklet chained to the wall. It was a street-by-street listing of surnames by house number. So I asked him if he used the information when he was a young copper to trace villains. Dad said he was fifteen, and if he met a girl at the youth club once he knew her name, he could find her address and cycle past her house or drop an anonymous Valentine's card through her letterbox."

"What a rogue," said Gus, "no chance of that these days. Most churches are locked, and that information is only available on request to protect the individual."

"What about the library details from July 2011 we collected," said Luke. "That could give us several names to search. The two youngsters rebuked by Ursula might appear on that list. At least one of them had to be a member. If we find one name, we can follow up on which school they attended and whether they went on to university."

"We might learn why their name didn't appear on the 2011 Census, too," said Gus.

"I picked those records up the last thing on Wednesday," said Neil. "They're right here on my desk. Unfortunately, because of the door-to-door, I didn't get a chance to go through them yesterday."

"You and Luke can start now, then, Neil. Good hunting."

Gus remembered one of his mental notes. The car parking issue. He called Geoff Mercer.

"Good morning, Gus," said Geoff. "Is this good news on the Wakeley case? Solved it already?"

"I'd like to say we're there," said Gus, "but it's two steps forwards, three steps back at times. If someone thinks we're unduly quick in achieving results, you should remind them of our remit."

"I know, you get the murder file, and everything's there for you. The forensics, the door-to-door enquiries, and witness statements get handed to you on a plate. Sometimes they've done a reconstruction and broadcast it on Crimewatch. You have to loosen a few alibis, ask different questions, and come up with the culprit. Then, as soon as you point the finger at the villain, you swan off to the Waggon & Horses for a celebratory drink. The ACC passes everything you find onto the detective squad from the first investigation. Their task is to wrap things up and pass a winning package to the Crown Prosecution Service. It's a doddle. How you persuaded the ACC to get you back on such a cushy number beats me."

"If everybody could do what I do, then life would be much better," said Gus. "While you're feeling positive about the CRT's achievements, can I ask that you badger the local Council for two extra parking spaces? Alex is with you at present, and Blessing Umeh's car is in the garage getting repaired. So we'll be scrabbling for spaces among the masses in the next week or so."

"I suppose if you don't get those spaces, it will impact your high success rate?" said Geoff.

"That's a given, Geoff."

"Anything for a quiet life," said Geoff.

Gus waited for a few seconds expecting his friend to say something more, but the rest was silence. Gus decided he'd wait until he saw the new signage on the wall outside indicating the six Crime Review Team parking spots. One mental note ticked. If only he could remember the others.

"We've got something, guv," said Luke.

"That was quick, Luke. Where was it?"

"In August 2011, a library member called Caitlyn Bendick signed in a visitor during the school holidays."

"Bendick? He's the shipping magnate, isn't he?" said Gus. "Is Caitlyn a grandchild?"

"Neil's checking, guv."

"Who did Ms Bendick sign in?"

"It's unclear, guv, but it looks like F. Wardrip. I might be wrong. There's nobody with that surname living locally."

"Oh, you're wrong, alright," said Gus. "Wardrip was a serial killer in the States. He murdered five women in the mid-Eighties. Our killer has a sense of humour.

"James Bendick married for a second time, guv," said Neil. "Caitlyn is his only child. The family live on Castle Hill. Bendick retains properties in London and Monte Carlo. He bought the Mere home in 1995, and Caitlyn arrived in 1997. His second wife Catherine is an interior designer with a London store; she also owns a separate property in Gstaad, Switzerland."

"When you say family, you're using the term in its general sense, I presume," said Gus. "Caitlyn's father spends much of his time in London or the South of France. Her mother has an office in the city during the week and a pied-à-Terre during the skiing season. So where did they stash their only daughter during term time?"

"At the time of the library incident, Caitlyn was at Bruton School for Girls," said Blessing Umeh.

"Listening in again, Blessing, well done," said Gus. "How do we know that?"

"As soon as we heard the name, we looked for Caitlyn's Facebook account," said Lydia.

"You were right, guv," said Blessing. "the term fees are more than ten thousand pounds. There's a school next to the premises for younger girls. It won't surprise me if Caitlyn has been there since she was old enough for Preparatory school."

"Have you found any Mere-related sites that Caitlyn Bendick or her family might have frequented?"

"Her parents don't have a personal online presence," said Lydia. "They've both got websites and business accounts on Facebook and Instagram. Catherine uses Pinterest too. Caitlyn uses her social media accounts for the usual things. She follows her favourite pop stars and person-alities. On Facebook, Caitlyn has around eight hundred friends. We're isolating the young men based within a twenty-mile radius of Mere. We've found two Pages concen-trating on local news and gossip for the town. Mere Chat has around six hundred and fifty members, but the posts ceased in December 2012."

"Isn't that unusual?" asked Gus.

"Millions of people join Facebook and never post a thing, guv," said Neil. "Perhaps they can't work out how to use it, or they search for long-lost friends for a while and get fed up. An inactive account can sit there for years, and nobody does a thing. Who were the administrators for Mere

Chat? We could ask them why they stopped. Maybe they switched to the second one you mentioned?"

"You could be right, Neil. That page got set up on the eighteenth of January in 2013. It's got over four thousand members. It records at least fifty posts a day."

"That's a busy little community page," said Gus.

"The eighteenth of January was only two days after Ursula's murder," said Luke.

"Did you find the name of the administrator for Mere Chat, Blessing?" asked Gus.

"Arnold Friend," said Blessing. "The surname appears here and there in the town. I can't find an Arnold, though, at the moment."

"Interesting," said Gus. "Let me make a phone call. Meanwhile, get a list of those six hundred-odd names associated with the Chat group. Was Caitlyn Bendick a member? Are there others that might be relevant?"

"One thing was unusual, guv," said Blessing. "On this page type, the administrator or moderator generally has a photograph of themselves on display. The header image might be a local landmark or an aerial shot of the town. That's what they had, but Arnold Friend chose a traditional depiction of Michael in full battle gear, his sword drawn ready for the coming battle."

"As in Michael, the avenging archangel?" asked Gus.

"Yes, guv. The archangels were the first angels created by God. Traditionally there were twelve, and they were sometimes associated with punishing wrongdoers."

Chapter Twelve

"URSULA WAS LIKE HER FATHER, Gideon. She saw it as
her role to confront wickedness wherever she saw it,"
said Gus.

"Here, the wrongdoers were the first to strike a blow,"
said Neil.

"Keep digging, Blessing," said Gus. "I'll make that call
now."

Gus called Horace Plant.

"Good morning, Mr Plant. Gus Freeman here. What
can you tell me about a gentleman called Arnold Friend?"

"He worshipped at our church, Mr Freeman. Before my
time, though. Did you visit our graveyard after we spoke?"

"No, we returned to our car after visiting a town café.
Why?"

"The Friend family has had its roots in the town for
generations, Mr Freeman. They were here before the
Wakeley family. Arnold Friend's gravestone is two plots to
the left of Gideon and Elspeth Wakeley. I believe he died in
1884."

"You told me that the early Methodists favoured a simpler form of religion," said Gus. "I assume his headstone is a basic slab or cross?"

"Oh no, Mr Freeman, Arnold Friend, was wealthy. The stone image of St Michael dominates that corner of the graveyard."

"Many thanks, Mr Plant," said Gus, "and goodbye."

Blessing and Lydia were watching Gus. It was clear they were waiting for something.

"Our avenging angel died in 1884," said Gus, "and is buried close to Brother Gideon. I don't think there's much doubt that Ursula set up the Mere Chat account to attract as many residents as possible. The Facebook page gave her access to shared gossip and the ability to snoop around online with no one realising. Ursula did that while in the library's telecentre."

"I wonder why the locals didn't suss that the person running the page wasn't a real member of the Friend family," said Neil.

"Perhaps they were more interested in the content," said Blessing. "People who joined the page posted many old photographs and revived long-lost memories. A memory from someone you hadn't seen in a while would be of more interest than checking out who created the page."

"Who manages the account that started just after Ursula's death?" Luke asked Blessing.

"Catherine Bendick is one of three people who now administer and moderate the page. Of course, that doesn't mean she was in from the start. People swap around from time to time due to pressure of work, illness, or simply moving out of the area."

"We need to ask the question of Mrs Bendick, Blessing," said Gus.

"I've transcribed a third of the members' names, guv," said Lydia. "It will take me a while."

"Get one of the lads to help," said Gus. "Blessing, find a phone number for this place on Castle Hill in Mere. I wonder whether Catherine Bendick is at home today. It's Friday morning, so she'll be in her London office. Perhaps they have a maid?"

"Do you want me to speak to her?" asked Blessing.

"It's the wife we want, Blessing. So, either you'll speak to her direct, or you'll badger the maid until she supplies the number of her employer's London office."

"Got it, guv."

"You have three questions when you get through to her. First, who came up with the idea of getting involved in the Mere Village Voice or whatever quaint name they chose? Then ask Catherine for the usual residential address of her husband. The last question will start alarm bells ringing. We need to know who slept at Castle Hill on the night of Wednesday, the sixteenth of January 2013. Tell her it's just a routine enquiry. Be creative. Don't give any hint we suspect her daughter of anything."

Blessing noted the list of questions and sought the phone number.

"That's why we couldn't trace the daughter via the Census data," said Luke. "Caitlyn was at school in Bruton, although we didn't have that information then, and the family address can't be in Mere. James and Catherine spend such a considerable amount of time elsewhere. Their regis-tered address could be anywhere."

"True, Luke. How many photographs are there on Cait-lyn's social media pages, Lydia?" asked Gus.

"Hundreds, guv,"

"Grab images of her facing the camera around the time

of the murder and something recent. Then we can get Ormrod and Dillon to confirm we've got our girl. Mrs Butterworth, Mrs Atkins, and Becky Burden would provide the icing on the cake if we showed the photos to them afterwards."

"We still have little on her companion, guv," said Neil.

"I thought you girls updated your profiles, you know, 'in a relationship' or something similar," said Luke.

"Always a mistake, Luke," said Lydia. "It turns sour within a month if you brag about it to your friends. And blokes you hoped might be interested in you disappear without a trace. It's always best to hedge your bets."

"Caitlyn and her mystery man were together from a young age if we've got the right couple," said Neil.

"I've trawled through her eight hundred friends on Facebook," said Lydia. "There's nothing to suggest any of the boys in her photos is her boyfriend. With the history they have between them, they made sure their online posts were neutral. They gave nothing away."

"I'll bet the boyfriend took the photos where she's face-on to the camera," said Luke.

"That's a creepy thought," said Lydia. "I've just copied three images he might have taken. What if he took photos at the bungalow in Shaftesbury Road, guv?"

"If he did, we'd find them when we catch him," said Gus. "It's not unusual for serial killers to keep trophies to relive the events."

Lunchtime came and went. Lydia and Neil completed the transcription of the members on the Mere Chat page. Luke had taken over from Lydia and was reducing Caitlyn's eight hundred Facebook friends to find males of the right age.

Gus walked over to sit beside Blessing. She was still on

the phone. Was this progress at last? Blessing thanked Mrs Bendick and ended the call.

"Right, guv. Did you know that Bendick is the Scottish variant of Benedict?"

Gus shook his head.

"James Bendick's registered address was where he lived with his first wife for years. It's in Rothesay, on the Isle of Bute. Caitlyn Bendick's details went there during the relocation exercise at the 2011 Census. That was an oversight. As for the Admin role on the town's gossip page, Catherine said Caitlyn urged her to get involved in local matters. When she went to university, Caitlyn wanted to keep in touch, and the old page wasn't functioning anymore. The last question threw her as you suspected, but after several minutes checking her diaries, she confirmed that the house was empty."

"Did Catherine offer any information on where Caitlyn studied after Bruton?" asked Gus.

"Caitlyn studied Politics and International Studies at the University of Warwick," said Blessing. "That was a three-year course which ended in the summer of 2017."

"That's where your father worked," said Gus, "do you think he knew her?"

"Out of twenty thousand students, guv?" said Blessing. "unlikely, he's a Computer Science Professor."

"No wonder you're so good at this stuff," said Gus.

"I'll dig deeper into Mere Chat, guv, to see whether Ursula contacted anyone direct as Arnold Friend. I'll give you an update before we finish today."

"Excellent," said Gus.

He moved across to his left, where Lydia was grafting away.

"Can you pass me copies of the images we need to put

before our Ringwood shopkeepers and the three ladies from Mere?"

"Yes, guv. Who do you want to make that trip?"

"Neil? Get your skates on. Mere, Ringwood and back with written confirmation that Caitlyn Bendick is our girl. Anything else you learn will be a bonus."

"Okay, guv. I'll see you at around four o'clock."

Neil collected the images from Lydia and agreed that they were clear enough for anyone to identify their suspect aged fifteen, eighteen and twenty. In the last picture, Caitlyn wore a broad smile and a striped scarf in the University of Warwick colours over a winter coat.

"Here's a message, guv," said Blessing. Gus stood behind her and looked over her shoulder.

The hand of the diligent will rule. The slothful will be put to forced labour

"Who received that message?"

"A man in his thirties, a labourer, unmarried, and unemployed at regular intervals by the look of it. If you read his posts, he follows Chelsea football, likes a drink, and swears a lot. The message came from the Avenging Angel. Ursula set up the Arnold Friend account to allow her to start the Mere Chat page, and then she accepted members as the administrator. When she wanted to send the equivalent of an old poison pen letter, she created another persona using A Friend but with the username of the Avenging Angel. Ursula used the same image for both accounts."

"The Moving Finger," said Gus, "Suzie talked me through the Agatha Christie story on Wednesday night."

"I haven't read that one," said Blessing.

"Keep searching," said Gus. "There's nothing aimed at Caitlyn or another well-educated male student yet."

"Maybe Ursula didn't send them a message, guv," said

Blessing. "If these two were evil from birth, they didn't need a trigger."

Luke clicked his fingers. He'd realised something.

"Why wasn't Caitlyn in Bruton that night? It was midweek, and they'd returned to school by around the fifth or sixth. So now I know why you told Blessing to ask who slept in the Mere house."

"Caitlyn faked an illness or a family emergency," said Gus, "this was well-planned from the outset. Her partner probably drove to Bruton to collect her. That's another angle we can pursue—young men who passed their driving test soon after their seventeenth birthday. The car could be distinctive if the lad were from a rich family. Start hunting."

"Surely, we need to find where Caitlyn Bendick is now, guv," said Lydia. "and get her taken into custody?"

"Caitlyn and her partner in crime were joined at the hip at least since they were fourteen," said Gus. "Wherever they are now, I guess they'll be together or in close contact. The last thing I want is to risk spooking her accomplice. He'll disappear. No, speed is of the essence, Lydia. We're getting closer every hour; I can feel it. We need to press on with analysing the material we have."

At a quarter past two, Gus heard an excited squeal.

"Here we are," said Blessing.

"Read it out," said Gus, "what did it say and who received it?"

I do not fear your threats. I am not frightened.

"That's a revision of a quote from St Peter, guv," said Blessing. "Our Avenging Angel sent it to Caitlyn Bendick on Sunday, the sixteenth of December 2012."

"We need to check with Becky Burden," said Gus, "but that could be twenty-four hours after the incident outside the café. Please tell me there were two recipients, Blessing."

"It will appear on the same day, so it won't take long for me to trace it," she replied.

"I've got a list of new driving licences issued for 2012, guv," said Luke. "I'm selecting the youngest names. I'll have a shortlist for you in the next few minutes."

"Dominic Hurley," said Blessing five minutes later.

"Dominic Hurley's on my list too, guv," said Luke, "passed his test in March 2012, five days after his seventeenth birthday."

"Hurley?" said Gus, "that can't be a coincidence. What was the name of the financier Ursula crossed swords with over the footpath issue?"

"Gervase Hurley, guv," said Luke, "he owns a large estate near Gillingham."

"I've found Dominic's Facebook account, guv," said Lydia. "He drives an Audi R8 Spyder. He looks pleased with himself, leaning on the driver's door."

"Is that a distinctive enough car for you? I assume his online profile is as bland as Caitlyn's?" said Gus.

"Hundreds of apparent friends, plenty of photos," said Lydia, "The images are similar to Caitlyn's. Here I am at so-and-so, but no sign of the anonymous person behind the camera. Dominic lists The Sherborne School and the University of Warwick under Education."

"No big surprise there. What did Dominic study?" asked Gus.

"He received a first-class degree in Economics in the summer of 2017," said Lydia.

"Hold on," said Blessing, "that's a three-year course. If Dominic was seventeen in 2012, he surely finished his A-levels at Sherborne in the summer of 2013. Six months after the murder."

"Is there any evidence that Dominic and Caitlyn took a gap year?" asked Gus.

"I'll need to scroll through these photos, guv," said Lydia. "If they were away for a year, I'd expect loads of photos, but only a handful appear on Dominic's account. I'll check Caitlyn's and get back to you."

"Arnold Friend sent another message to Dominic Hurley, guv, on New Year's Day," said Blessing.

"Just to Dominic? OK, read it out."

Your eye is evil. Your entire body is full of darkness.

"Ursula understood what evil Dominic was capable of, didn't she? That message prompted the plan to kill her. We can only guess. But maybe Ursula overheard Dominic and Caitlyn talking about acting out their fantasies at the library. That's what they were at that stage, the fantasies of two young teenagers whose families had showered them with money but never affection. Ursula was the first murder they committed together. Now we need to find the other victims and ensure no more women get killed."

"I've found a blank period in the dates on Caitlyn's photos, guv. There were no posts between March and August 2014. I'll double-check Dominic's details."

"What does that suggest, Luke?" asked Gus.

"Over the years, travel firms have developed a series of backpacking tours that let students visit popular spots in South East Asia, guv. They spent a month each in Thailand, Laos, Cambodia, and Vietnam, then came back via the States or had a beach holiday en route to the UK."

"The Maldives," said Lydia, "I've found a photo posted on Dominic's page on August the third, 2014."

"Why so few photos?" asked Gus.

"They may have thought it was cheaper to use a digital camera rather than their mobile phone for hundreds of shots," said Lydia. "Then, when they got home, the hassle of loading them onto their computer proved too much. Especially as they were getting ready to go to university in September."

"We must pass this link to Geoff Mercer," Gus said. "I bet that not posting holiday snaps was more about not leaving a trail that pinned them in a specific location. That backpacking trip could have seen their next kill or kills."

"So, in September 2014, they started at the University of Warwick," said Luke. "Where have they been since they left in the summer of 2017? Where are they now?"

"I'm keen to hear what Alex discovers," said Gus. "he's due here in ninety minutes."

"I can see why Hurley chose Warwick," said Blessing. "Oxford and Cambridge have top-ranking, but my father says that Warwick is in what they term the magic circle of universities for investment banking and other highly competitive employment centres."

"Dominic planned to follow in his father's footsteps," said Lydia.

"Caitlyn's second-class degree might allow her to find a position at Westminster," said Luke. "It would allow them to live and work together in the capital."

Lydia, Luke, and Blessing continued to gather evidence. Gus updated his copy of the Freeman Files. Finally, they were getting close to the end. Or was it the end of the beginning?

At a quarter to four, Gus heard the lift descend to the ground floor.

It was Neil Davis.

"I hope you stayed within the speed limit, Neil," said Gus.

"Most of the time, guv. When someone was watching, at least."

"You've brought us good news, I hope?"

"The best, guv. Each of our five witnesses identified Caitlyn Bendick as the girl in question. Becky Burden told me that the young man outside the café window was a familiar sight in town. He drove an Audi R8 Spyder, even though he was only a kid, and she thought his father was a big wig who lived in Gillingham, five miles up the road."

"Dominic Hurley," said Gus, "the son of the wealthy financier, Gervase Hurley."

"Oh, you knew already. That bloke who bought the land behind Ursula's bungalow," said Neil, "and wanted the foot-path removed."

"The very same, Neil. It fits, doesn't it? Hurley started it off when he bought the land. Bendick came on the scene five years later. Ursula Wakeley irritated both men by objecting to their plans at every opportunity. When she saw Caitlyn and Dominic at the library, she couldn't resist picking on them. The incident Mrs Atkins saw might not have been the first. The eerie part is that Ursula recognised the evil within Dominic purely by being in his presence. Maybe she saw something in Caitlyn too. We don't understand the true dynamic between the pair yet."

"Mrs Atkins said Caitlyn laughed in Ursula's face," said Neil. "Dominic was a tall lad, even at fifteen. He towered over Ursula. When I showed Mrs Atkins the photo this afternoon, she remembered the young man's face as he glared at Ursula. It surprised her Ursula didn't turn to stone. Dominic gave her such a wicked look."

"I've been updating my digital files," said Gus. "The others will soon do the same. They're just completing the evidence-gathering from social media accounts."

"I'll get my files updated, guv," said Neil. "I'll grab a coffee first if that's okay?"

"Since you offered, Neil," said Lydia. "None of them has had time this afternoon. The usual for us, and when Alex arrives, it's…."

"White, one sugar," said Neil, "I remember."

The team continued working as the clock ticked on.

Alex Hardy arrived at four twenty-five.

"You look busy," he said, "I thought you would wind down for the weekend."

"We've had a breakthrough, Alex," said Gus, "unfortunately, it may only be a reprieve. What did you find?"

"You were right, as usual, guv," said Alex. He took the empty chair next to Gus and opened a file.

"An eighty-one-year-old widow, Katherine McKenna, died in 2015. The victim received fourteen stab wounds from two separate blades. A seven-inch plain-edged blade was the murder weapon, and a four-inch serrated blade did most of the damage post-mortem."

"Where did the victim live?" asked Gus.

"Measham, a large village beyond Nuneaton," said Alex.

"That places it around thirty miles northwest of Coventry and the University of Warwick," said Blessing.

"Tiny town, a large village," said Gus, "It fits with their hunting ground. Any other similarities to our victim."

"Katherine McKenna suffered from glaucoma, guv. They had registered her blind since 2013."

"East Midlands police cover that area," said Gus, "did you learn how they handled the case there?"

"Her son, who lived in Leicester, reported the theft of several items. He estimated the value at around ten thousand pounds. The detectives brought in likely suspects making no progress. They never found the stolen gear nor the weapons used."

"What did the detective in charge think had happened?" asked Gus.

"She thought it was robbery with violence at first, guv. Then when they couldn't link any of the likely lads to the investigation, she assumed a random pair of druggies butchered Mrs McKenna."

"Of course they did. Then left the police with zero forensics. The killers were professionals, while the detectives were amateurs. So why didn't they link this case to Ursula Wakeley?"

"Probably for the same reason that they didn't link it to Maisie Fletcher, guv,"

"Who?" said Gus. "When was that?"

"The following year, around eighteen months after Mrs McKenna. Maisie was seventy-seven, another widow, but this time she lived in the West Midlands. A place called Cheswick Green. That's near Solihull and less than twenty miles from Coventry."

"Same modus operandi, Alex?" asked Neil.

"A further escalation in violence," said Alex. Gus sat back in his chair. This was what he feared.

"Maisie Fletcher had been profoundly deaf from birth," said Alex. "She lived a full life, married, and had three children. She worked as a catering assistant until she retired, aged seventy-three, in 2012. Her husband, Stan, died in 2015. The house was in a rural setting, and police believe the property was under observation for some time. Maisie had lots of visitors, both family and friends. It was unusual for her to be alone for any length of time. The break-in took place during the night, perhaps as late as midnight. When her daughter arrived the following afternoon, she entered a scene that she could only describe as a nightmare. There was blood in every room of the house. The killers appear to have moved Maisie from room to room, cutting her, then applying a tourniquet using strips they cut from her night-dress. The police surgeon estimated the time of death as between seven and nine in the morning. They tormented Maisie for hours."

"Was there any deviation in the weapon?" asked Gus.

"From the description of the wounds, both assailants used different weapons from the McKenna murder. However, as the cases never got linked, nobody compared the wounds. In addition, nobody has examined the crime scene evidence to see whether the same pair were responsible."

"How did West Midlands classify it?" asked Gus.

"There was nothing taken, guv, no forensics, no sexual assault, and nobody suspicious hanging around. Maisie Fletcher didn't have an enemy in the world. So what do we do in such cases?"

"Clutch at straws," said Gus.

"They clutched for around five weeks and then gave up the ghost."

"Do we have everything recorded in the Freeman Files?" he asked the team.

"Yes, guv," came the united response.

"Right, that's as far as we can take things for today. I suggest you get off home for the weekend. Do something different from searching for clues to bloody murders."

"I get it, guv," said Luke, "it's someone else's job now to find Bendick and Hurley and arrest them. We've established their connection to Ursula Wakeley. We understand that her religious zeal contributed to her demise. What made these two the way they are will be for others to decide."

"Few serial killers work in tandem," said Gus. "We have examples in recent history where couples acted together: Brady and Hindley, Fred, and Rose West spring to mind. There is always one dominant partner acting with a submissive. That relationship was changing based on the murders this couple committed in 2015 and 2016. We can't know the nature of any murders in South East Asia until checks are made. Maybe they took a gap year. If the trend from 2016 continued in the past two years, Caitlyn would now be dominant. She will kill for Dominic. That's the nature of the beast."

"It's a horrid thought, guv," said Lydia.

"Bendick and Hurley have no sense of right and wrong. Ursula spotted that. They only have a tenuous grasp of human emotions. Dominic realised that Caitlyn would do anything he asked of her. That feeling of power over someone is addictive. That was another reason I didn't chase after Caitlyn Bendick the second we identified her. Dominic Hurley has a taste for power now. He would want the thrill of finding a new accomplice. Someone he could dominate in the way he dominated Caitlyn."

"I can see the ad in the paper now, guv," said Neil: "Help wanted. Masks supplied. No previous experience necessary."

"He's a monster, Neil," said Lydia. "How can you be so flippant?"

"It takes practice, Lydia. It's a release mechanism. Without it, I'd never leave here and act normally when I got home to Melody. My Dad drank to forget. So I opted for gallows humour. I never had the benefits of a university education, but I had a loving family like you. Bendick and Hurley had wealthy parents who sent them away to the best schools. All that privilege, and what did they do? They took exception to Ursula Wakeley's comments and taught her a lesson. If they possessed a shred of humanity, they would have compared their start in life with hers and realised how lucky they were. Her strict, spartan upbringing was light-years from the cosseted childhood those two enjoyed. Ursula used to talk about the risks of sparing the rod. She and her brother, Arthur, had to cut the switches themselves from the trees behind the bungalow for their father Gideon to punish them."

"Do you think Bendick and Hurley would have turned out better if they had suffered physical abuse as they did, Neil?" asked Gus.

"I've no idea, guv," said Neil. "But it might make me feel better if they suffered when someone catches up with them. Those crime scene photos on the board will stay with me for ages."

"Think yourself lucky you haven't seen Maisie Fletcher's then, Neil," said Alex.

"What a week," said Gus. "Get off home. I'll talk to DS Mercer and the ACC. First, they need to decide who should carry this case forward. Then, they'll do the necessary if it's still on their desk on Monday morning. I don't have a warrant card, so someone with one will arrest Bendick and Hurley wherever they are. Their reign of silent terror is coming to a close."

Epilogue

"RIGHT THEN, ALEX," said Gus. "What else do you have for me now the others have gone?"

"The broad description I'm using for our suspect on the Hub's data is throwing up dozens of recorded sightings. I'll need more time to confirm which ones are relevant. But I have a hunch our red-headed sniper links to several incidents in the past."

"I suspected as much," said Gus, "and it's no surprise you're getting alternatives. We're guessing at an age range."

"I'll keep digging next week, guv. One sighting looks promising. In September 2012, a Nigerian cultural attaché died in suspicious circumstances. His name was Solomon Okonkwo, and he lived in a penthouse apartment in Marylebone. Okonkwo fell from a window, and his naked body landed on the street below. Fortunately, nobody got in his way. The police couldn't find evidence of foul play; at first, they believed it was a tragic accident. However, despite the Nigerian High Commission's attempts to sweep the matter under the diplomatic carpet, investigative reporters uncovered another story. A young domestic servant who worked for Okonkwo committed suicide by swallowing bleach earlier in the year. Olabisi Promise Chukwu was just twelve years old when she got trafficked to Britain. Behind closed doors, she got raped and beaten. Okonkwo threatened to throw her into the street when she asked for a day's holiday when she was fourteen. Olabisi returned to household duties and submitted whenever he wanted her. Migrant domestic workers are in a uniquely vulnerable position. Thousands of miles from home, they rely on that single employer for their accommodation, work, and immigration status. An older woman employee came forward after the attaché's death to tell Olabisi's story."

"How did the police connect the red-headed man to this case?" asked Gus.

"When they asked residents of the apartments if they'd seen anyone that day, a Post Office employee overheard a conversation. She described a man with a high-viz waistcoat and a clipboard, claiming he came from the local council. He said there had been complaints from residents on the top floor about pigeons in the loft space."

"A likely tale," said Gus, "but it got him into the building."

"Okonkwo returned to his apartment late in the afternoon. The man that the postwoman saw was in the apartment for several hours."

"The method he used to get rid of a criminal who felt himself above the law differed greatly from the Burnside killing," said Gus, "but I can't argue with the sentiment. So how can we be sure it's the same man, Alex?"

"We can't on the evidence I've gathered so far, guv. Our red-headed man acted alone on both occasions. Is that because he's a loner? Or a gun for hire? Does he work within an organisation? I need to connect him to other people. I'll get there, but it will take time."

"Fair enough," said Gus, "we'll meet again same time next week."

Alex left Gus in the office and chased after Lydia. They were in for a busy weekend.

Gus called Geoff Mercer and arranged to meet him at half-past ten in the morning at London Road.

It was six before he left the Old Police Station office and headed for Urchfont. Suzie arrived before him. She was inside preparing dinner.

"That smells lovely," he said, "is this a special occasion?"

"Are you going to the allotment in the morning?" asked Suzie.

"I'm planning on working in the afternoon," said Gus. "I've got an appointment with Geoff Mercer at half-past ten. I'm handing over everything we gathered on the Ursula Wakeley case."

Gus explained the events of the past two days over dinner. Then, as they went to the bedroom later that evening, he remembered her earlier question.

"Why did you want to know about my plans for the morning?" he asked.

"There are things I need to collect from home," said Suzie.

"If they need two of us to fetch them, then tonight was a special occasion," said Gus. "I'll cancel my trip to the allotment. Then, I'm all yours after I get back from London Road."

"That was the idea," said Suzie.

Saturday, 7 July 2018

GUS TOOK Geoff Mercer through the details of the Wakeley case, and he agreed to set the wheels in motion straight away.

"The sooner they're found, the better. I'll get Bendick and Hurley under observation until we can grab both simultaneously. What is it with you, Gus? We hand you a tricky murder case, and you unmask two serial killers."

"It's not deliberate, Geoff. But, look, don't lose sight of the Asian angle. Pass the details on to the authorities in the areas concerned. We know the specific time frame. Let's hope Bendick and Hurley went on holiday and nothing else."

Gus and Suzie spent the afternoon moving the last of her things from Worton to Urchfont.

John and Jackie Ferris seemed upbeat.

They even reminded them of the invitation to Sunday lunch.

"Blessing's parents are coming to inspect her lodgings," said John.

"I see," said Gus, "you want reinforcements."

"Not us," said Jackie, "It's Blessing; she's petrified."

Sunday, 8 July 2018

BLESSING UMEH WAS awake at dawn. After breakfast, she walked around the farm. It seemed so quiet. It would be a shame if her father thought it unsuitable.

Blessing's mobile phone rang.

"Hello, Blessing? It's Dave here, Dave Smith."

It was the hunky PC with the cornflower blue eyes. Oh yes, Blessing remembered.

"Is it my car?" said Blessing. "Did the garage fail to fix it, and they asked you to break the news?"

"No, it will be ready on Thursday. What if I help my brother-in-law by delivering it to you? Perhaps we could go out for the evening, and then I can get a taxi back to Chippenham?"

"That sounds great," said Blessing. "I'll see you on Thursday evening."

Well, that was an excellent start to the day, thought Blessing. Long may it continue.

Monday, 9 July 2018

WHEN GUS ARRIVES at the office, he receives an update on the Wakeley case from Geoff Mercer.

"Good morning, Gus," said Geoff. "I have news I'm sure you want to hear. The Metropolitan Police arrested Dominic Hurley and Caitlyn Bendick at an apartment in Chelsea Village on Sunday evening. Hurley's first request was for his solicitor. He never once mentioned his parents."

"Did he say anything more?" asked Gus.

"We constantly thought about getting caught," said Geoff, "but the rush was worth the risk."

"That's a quote," said Gus, "not Wardrip this time, but I've read it somewhere."

"Caitlyn Bendick didn't utter a word until the officers separated the couple and led them to the lift," said Geoff. "Then she turned to the officers, and with a broad smile, she told them, you can never separate us from our memories."

"They were as evil as one another," said Gus. "if only we could have stopped them earlier."

THE ACC CALLED LATER to add his congratulations and asked Gus to get to London Road at noon. He had another cold case to hand over.

GUS HAD news of his own to tell the team.

Alex and Lydia will be keen to tell the others what they learned at the weekend.

Every week provides new challenges for Gus Freeman and the Crime Review Team.

Why would this week be any different?

vinci-books.com/nighttrain

Secrets, lies, and a killer on the loose. Can Gus Freeman unravel the truth?

As the Crime Review Team investigate the puzzling death of Ivan Kendall and close in on a ruthless assassin, an old adversary resurfaces, determined to derail their progress. With personal revelations complicating matters, the team must navigate treacherous waters to uncover the truth.

Turn the page for a free preview…

Night Train: Chapter One

Saturday, 8 March 2014

Ivan Kendall lived in Pontyclun, a village twelve miles from Cardiff. He was self-employed and ran a modest window cleaning business he'd developed since getting made redundant from a building materials supplier in 2008. Ivan had joined the company straight from school at sixteen.

Ivan was forty-five years old and married to Sally, his childhood sweetheart. Their daughter Alexa attended Y Pant Comprehensive on the Cowbridge Road and was weeks away from sitting her Year 11 exams. Alexa's ambition was to leave school and go to college in Bridgend. A fifteen-minute train journey allowed her to study at the Hair and Beauty Academy before starting her own mobile hairdressing business. Her mother, Sally, had left school at fifteen and worked as a shop assistant in various stores ever since, except for her six-month maternity leave.

Ivan, Sally, and Alexa lived in a three-bedroomed semi-detached house they rented from the local council. A life less ordinary would be hard to imagine. It was a constant battle for Ivan Kendall to keep his head above water.

His neighbours knew him as a quiet man who wore a distinctive salt-and-pepper beard. However, the stress the family experienced following Ivan's redundancy and the constant economic pressure meant those neighbours would freely admit that Ivan and Sally had a stormy relationship. Since 2008, the couple had separated on three occasions.

First, Sally left to go a few miles away to stay with her mother in Llanharry, taking Alexa with her. She returned after six weeks. In 2010, she moved to a gastropub in Cardiff to work as a barmaid. Ivan looked after Alexa alone. While in Cardiff, Sally started a relationship with the bar owner, Thomas Griffiths. Tommy was fifty-five, hard-working, and cared deeply for Sally.

On this occasion, it was eight months before Sally gave her marriage another chance. She moved back into the house in Pontyclun just before Christmas. Everything was sweetness and light in the Kendall household throughout 2011 and 2012.

The third and final time Sally left Ivan was in the summer of 2013. Once again, she ran away to stay with her mother. Within a month, Tommy Griffiths left his Cardiff pub and rented a flat in the village. Everyone realized Tommy wanted to take Sally away from Pontyclun for good. An uneasy period followed when Tommy Griffiths left Pontyclun and took over a busy bar on the seafront in Weymouth. Sally returned to Ivan a week later.

Saturday, the eighth of March, started as an ordinary day for the Kendall family. Ivan left in his white van at eight in the morning to visit six properties on his window cleaning round. Sally knew to expect him home by half-past twelve.

He would hand over most of the cash he'd earned and keep a few pounds back for himself.

While Ivan was out of the house, Sally got the washing up together and persuaded Alexa to help tidy the house. Ivan went to the rugby club on Saturday afternoons to watch a match and have a few beers. Sally and Alexa would visit the local supermarkets seeking bargains that eked out the pennies towards another week's food shopping.

It was rare for Ivan and Sally to venture out in the evenings. Alexa drifted around the village with friends. Her parents didn't know half of what she got up to and didn't seem that bothered as long as Alexa got home by ten o'clock.

Tonight there was a change in their predictable routine. Ivan had been later returning from the rugby club than usual. Sally could tell it wasn't because he'd kept drinking. Her husband was sober and yet was on edge. He couldn't settle for watching television for more than a few minutes. Sally didn't want to start an argument, so she held her tongue.

At half-past eight, Ivan left the living room and went upstairs. He came down ten minutes later and went out. As the door slammed behind him, Sally couldn't have known it was the last time she would see him alive.

Alexa crept in a few minutes after ten and looked in on her mother. She still had her scarf wrapped around her neck. Sally knew what that meant. She'd suffered enough love-bites in her teens. Sally prayed that whoever Alexa had been with used protection.

"Where's Dad gone?" asked Alexa.

"He didn't say," said her mother. "He will have gone to the rugby club or a pub in town, I expect. There was something on his mind."

"No," said Alexa, "we were near the station when I spotted him. He never saw us, but he got on the Cardiff train at five to nine."

"That doesn't sound right," said Sally. "He'll have to get a taxi home. I've no idea how he could afford that. What's his game?"

Alexa went to her bedroom. Sally tried to watch television but couldn't concentrate. She followed Alexa upstairs by half-past ten and fell asleep without hearing a key in the door.

Sunday, 9th March 2014

Westbury is a station managed by Great Western Railway that services a market town on the north-western edge of Salisbury Plain. It lies near the border with Somerset. Westbury is famous for the White Horse cut into the chalk face of the hillside above the town in the early eighteenth century. Murder is a rare commodity in this quiet corner of the county.

The station is a major junction, serving the Reading to Taunton line with services to and from London Paddington and Penzance in Cornwall. There are also mainline services to and from Portsmouth, Cardiff, and Swindon. In addition, local services from Bristol Temple Meads to Weymouth, plus services to London Waterloo, are available. For a town with a population of only eighteen thousand, including the numerous surrounding villages, it's a station that punches well above its weight.

Sid Dyer was a conductor who lived on the outskirts of town in Westbury Leigh and started his shift at six o'clock. He parked his 125cc motorcycle in the car park, securing it with a chain to a large steel hoop set into the ground. He had thirty-five minutes before his first train arrived. Sid would cover the journey to Castle Cary and Taunton and switch trains returning through Westbury on the morning train that ferried passengers to the capital. He'd worked on the railways since leaving school. Nothing much surprised Sid Dyer. He'd seen all sorts over the years.

His first port of call was the Gents. At sixty-three, Sid knew the benefits of visiting the toilet whenever the opportunity presented itself. The platform near the main station buildings was deserted early in the day. The solid-looking red brick construction stood on this spot for over a century. Sid sensed something different to the thousands of other occasions he'd walked this platform as soon as he pushed open the door to the public convenience.

Each of the stalls was available, and there was nobody else inside. Yet as he stood at the urinal, Sid couldn't relax and kept glancing over his shoulder. Why was he so nervous? Sid washed his hands and dried them. He paid closer attention to the stalls.

When he pushed the end door open further, he saw the blood.

"Well, Sidney," he sighed. "I reckon you must wait for the Penzance train to rattle into the station before you get any conductor duties done today. There's far too much blood for there not to be a body somewhere. Time to call the police, I reckon."

Two local uniformed officers arrived by car, and a forensic crew and a detective soon followed. As the officers searched the station for a victim, the toilets were closed for the Crime Scene Investigators to do their stuff.

Sid Dyer sat in the station's award-winning buffet with a mug of coffee, telling a DC Trainer everything he knew.

The young man was green as grass, and Sid knew that he didn't know about the railways or how they operated.

"There was nobody on the platform when you arrived, and you didn't pass anyone in Station Approach as you rode in?" asked DC Trainer.

"I didn't see anyone on foot between Westbury Leigh and here. Nobody passed me in a car or van before you ask. If a bloke was staggering around in the town covered in blood, someone might have called you, don't you think?"

"How far is Westbury Leigh from here? One mile?"

"That's right. I used to walk to work in the old days, but when I've been on my feet all day walking up and down the corridors, I need to ride home."

"How did this supposed victim get here?" asked DC Trainer.

"It's not for me to tell you your job," said Sid, "but there was a lot of blood in that end stall. Dried blood. So, you need the answer to two questions. First, where did someone move him last night after they attacked him? Second, on which train did he arrive?"

"When did the last train stop here last night?" asked DC Trainer.

"The 21.30 from Cardiff pulled in around 23.45. The night trains you might have seen in the black-and-white films still exist, but they're few and far between these days. That train is as close to midnight as we get at Westbury. The Riviera Sleeper leaves London Paddington at around a quarter to midnight, but apart from Reading, its next stop is Taunton."

DC Trainer left Sid Dyer to finish his coffee. He went to find the forensic crew. Perhaps they could convince him this wasn't a waste of a Sunday morning. Instead, he soon learned their mystery man had been attacked by at least two men in the Gents' toilet. There were signs of a struggle outside the redbrick station building in the car park opposite where Sid Dyer parked his motorcycle. Scuff marks and blood spots showed someone got bundled into a vehicle and then left at speed.

When he returned to the police station, DC Trainer wondered how many stops there were between Cardiff and Westbury stations. It would be like finding a needle in a haystack. He had plenty of other things demanding his attention.

It might be quicker to wait for someone to call in about a missing person or for the blood results to come back. Then, with luck, they would match someone in the system. As for this Sunday afternoon, DC Clive Trainer had a date with England and Wales at Twickenham. It was England's first chance at a Triple Crown in eleven years.

In Pontyclun, Sally Kendall had waited all morning for Ivan to return. Alexa was still asleep. Sally wondered whether to phone the police. Had something happened to Ivan, or had he left her? She dialled 999 and reported him missing.

When Sid Dyer finished his shift in the early evening, he rode along Station Approach on his motorcycle. Where was the closest place to the station to dump a body? You would need somewhere it didn't get found right away. Sid slowed to turn right towards Westbury Leigh. Just ahead of him and to his left was Slag Lane, which led to the fishing lakes. They were as convenient a place as any. It was a muddy, boggy area with poor footpaths, although local councillors debated giving the popular amenity a much-needed face-lift. When he reached home, he called the number on the card DC Trainer had left on the buffet room table earlier that morning.

Monday, 10 March 2014

A diver discovered the body of a bearded man, aged between forty and fifty years of age, at half-past seven in the morning. Robbery didn't appear to be the reason for the attack. There was cash in the man's pockets, although he wasn't carrying credit cards, a mobile phone, or any means of identification. He had a return ticket to Cardiff Central and Pontyclun in his back trouser pocket.

The victim suffered severe head injuries before he got thrown into the lake. Whether blunt force trauma was the cause of death would depend on the post-mortem. DC Trainer stood at the side of the lake and reflected on what the forensic boys had told him. Two assailants sounded right. The guy on the plastic sheeting on the bank was a well-built, stocky individual. He wouldn't have given in without a fight, and it would take an enormous man to lift him in and out of the car before throwing him into the water. No, it made sense that they were looking for two assailants.

Who was the victim, and what was the motive? The tickets ruled out the station permutations he'd fretted over yesterday afternoon as he watched England demolish Wales. His boss was already on the phone with South Wales Police checking for reports of a loved one not returning home on Saturday night.

The South Wales police found it difficult to figure out why anyone wanted to kill this quiet family man. Ten days after the murder investigation began, officers arrested Tommy

Griffiths in Weymouth and charged him with the murder. The bar owner was later released and cleared of the allegations. Griffiths always denied claims he was involved. He told reporters that the police were desperate for a motive, and he was the only one available.

Sally Kendall also believed in Tommy's innocence and was quoted as saying that although Tommy and Ivan weren't friends, for obvious reasons, they weren't enemies either. Tommy knew she was returning to Ivan when she left him in Cardiff. He'd followed her to Pontyclun because he was in love with her, but he accepted that Sally would never leave her husband.

Sally's and Alexa's whereabouts by the end of 2014 were unknown. The lack of motive for the killing and the mystery behind his journey to Westbury that Saturday night made Sally fear for her life. Her neighbours saw little reason for that fear, but they, too, couldn't explain why Ivan Kendall did something so out of character.

As for Wiltshire Police, they dismissed the murder as being caused by mistaken identity. Someone knew Ivan Kendall was on that night train, and his destination was Westbury. Did he argue with fellow travellers, or were two men waiting for him to arrive? What could have been so essential to cause Ivan to travel eighty miles late at night with no explanation to his wife?

Two weeks after the murder, a security man on an industrial estate near Warminster reported an abandoned vehicle. He'd inspected the Toyota Yaris and spotted bloodstains around the nearside rear passenger window.

Three weeks later, the detective teams in Wiltshire and South Wales hoped a reconstruction of Ivan Kendall's last movements, starting from the approach to Pontyclun station, would jog someone's memory. They were mainly concerned about the two men in the Toyota Yaris in Westbury. But no one came forward. The Yaris had been stolen from a multi-storey car park in Bath on the seventh of March. There was no forensic evidence inside to identify the driver or his colleague.

Ivan Kendall's former workmates at the building merchants and customers on his window-cleaning round described him as a quiet chap who kept himself to himself. Officers travelled on trains on either side of the Bristol Channel, looking for passengers on the train that night. They showed pictures of Ivan, hoping someone might have seen something unusual.

The result was a familiar one. The murder appeared motiveless, the suspects never got identified, and the case disappeared into cold storage. DC Clive Trainer passed his sergeant's exams at the end of 2015 and transferred to Sussex Police based at their Headquarters in Lewes, East Sussex.

Sid Dyer retired at sixty-five in June 2016. On a stormy day in March of the following year, he got knocked from his 125cc motorcycle by a vehicle as he rode from Westbury Leigh into the town centre. He died in the ambulance en route to the Royal United Hospital in Bath.

Grab your copy...
vinci-books.com/nighttrain

About the Author

Ted Tayler is the international bestselling indie author of The Freeman Files and The Phoenix series. Ted lives in the English west country, where his stories are based. He was born in 1945 and has been married to Lynne since 1971. They have three children and four grandchildren.

His thought-provoking mysteries appeal to readers of Sally Rigby, Joy Ellis, Pauline Rowson, and Faith Martin. His action-packed thrillers are a must for fans of Mark Dawson and J. C. Ryan.

Gus Freeman's cold case investigations are carried out with reasoned deduction rather than bursts of frantic action. In each of the twenty-four books, unsolved murder is accompanied by romance, humor, and country life. The core message in the twelve Phoenix novels is that criminals should pay for their crimes. Unfortunately, the current system fails to deliver the correct punishment, so Phoenix helps redress the balance.

Acknowledgments

The love and support of my family; without them, this would have been impossible.